Here's what readers are saying about The Traveling Tea Ladies!

"As owner of The Tea Academy and Miss Melanie's Tea Room & Gourmet Tea Emporium, Melanie O'Hara has made a seamless foray into murder and mayhem set among tea enthusiasts in the South. Her primary women characters, Amelia, Olivia, Cassandra and Sarah, combine sophistication with compassion and eccentricity as they drink tea in Amelia's Victorian tea room, experiment with delectable recipes and juggle jobs, family, social calendars and shopping. Their trip from the sleepy town of Dogwood Cove, Tennessee, to the big city of Dallas for a girl's weekend exceeds their expectations for "adventure" when murder is unexpectedly added to the menu. In the tradition of the British cozy mystery, *The Traveling Tea Ladies* blends quirky characters, good food and drink with mystery and intrigue."

Judy Slagle, Department Chair of Literature and Languages
East Tennessee State Unviersity

"Melanie O'Hara opens the door on unexpected intrigue from the genteel tea rooms of East Tennessee. The mystery is steeped in local color as the tea ladies muster their forces to help a friend in need. Readers will want to put a pot on and do some traveling themselves."

Randall Brown, Writer, *Knoxville News Sentinel*

"Talk about a perfect book to read at the beach … entertaining and intriguing! Melanie O'Hara is a young woman whose background of owning a tea room has provided the perfect experiences for her unique books about *The Traveling Tea Ladies!*

The Traveling Tea Ladies Death in Dixie is a story that shows the deep friendships and loyalty of four friends who share an acute interest in tea. I found myself making notes of certain types of tea to try and could almost taste some of the tea foods and candy the author described.

This second book of Melanie's does make you wonder what can happen to these creative and resourceful women next. I can't wait—the next book will take place in Savannah!"

Kathy Knight
Accent Editor, *The Greeneville Sun*

"I guarantee that once you start this book, you will not be able to put it down. In fact, I was so connected to the storyline that I almost missed my train stop. Rarely do I find a book that can capture my attention so deeply that I forget I am riding to work on the noisy NYC subway. I highly recommend this book. It's perfect for a book club or to give your best friend as a gift. Every time I sat down to read this book, I felt I was getting together with my closest friends. It is a true gem indeed. I cannot wait to read about the next adventure The Traveling Tea Ladies take on."

Patty Aizaga, NYCGirlAtHeart.com

Melanie O'Hara

THE TRAVELING
TEA LADIES

Death in Dallas

LYONS
LEGACY
PUBLISHING™

Johnson City, Tennessee

The Traveling Tea Ladies™
Death in Dallas

Cover art by Susi Galloway
www.SusiGalloway.com

Book design by Longfeather Book Design
www.LongfeatherBookDesign.com

LYONS
LEGACY
PUBLISHING™

You may contact the publisher at:
Lyons Legacy Publishing™
123 East Unaka Aveneue
Johnson City, Tennessee 37601
Publisher@LyonsLegacyPublishing.com

ISBN: 978-0-9836145-4-8

For Essie
For showing us unconditional love,
Teaching us the power of forgiveness,
And making each of her grandchildren feel
As though we are her favorite!
I love you very much.

Acknowledgements

Endless thanks to my husband, Keith, my real-life "Shane Spencer." Thank you for always being my "Biggest Fan" and making all my dreams come true and for pushing me to finish this book.

To my children, Olivia and Charlie who make my heart sing! I so love being your Mom and have enjoyed every age and stage of your life. I am fiercely proud of the smart, beautiful and motivated young adults growing up before my eyes! Thank you both for allowing me to base a character on you.

Thank you to Susi Galloway for making "the ladies" come to life yet again!

Thanks to Erik Jacobson at Longfeather Book Design for your meticulous attention to detail. You rock!

And finally in memory of my grandmother, Frankie Lucille Wade, affectionately called Essie, who passed away this past June. She was able to read the first edition of this book and see the dedication to her. I miss her every day!

THE TRAVELING TEA LADIES

TEA LADIES

Death in Dallas

ONE

*I*t had been a long, hot and humid summer in Dogwood Cove, Tennessee. This summer had made the record books as the mercury continued to soar. It was the third year in a row the area had suffered a drought. The lack of rain had taken a toll on the strawberry, pumpkin, apple and tomato crops in the area which would mean a decrease in tourists during Dogwood Cove's Apple Festival.

Putting the tea room up for sale was something I never imagined I would be doing. I loved every inch of this regal pink beauty. Built in 1904, it had housed Dogwood Cove's first police chief and his seven children. Past families that had lived in the home had shared photos and tales of sliding down the great curved banister in the entry way. They had shown me the shoot at the back of the house where the coal trucks had made deliveries to keep the eight fireplaces heated. It was the second house built on the street, back when the road had been graveled and horse and buggies were the norm of transportation.

I was not looking forward to packing up all the antiques and belongings that filled our Victorian tea room. Any movement that required an extra ounce of exertion was sure to make beads of sweat pop out on my forehead. Moving is always a trial, no matter what time of year you plan a move, especially in late August!

"It's time to move on, Amelia," Shane conceded while taking another bite of homemade peanut butter pie. He gently put his arm around my shoulders and gave me a loving squeeze. "I know how hard this decision is on you, but I need your help in the business now. Remember, starting the wholesale company was your idea to make work easier on you." He quickly wiped the chocolate traces from his mouth with a satisfied smile on his face.

"I know," I said as my eyes filled with tears. "But the tea room has been a part of my after life and part of Dogwood Cove for so long. I have made lasting friendships with so many people over the years." I tried to smile as tears continued to spill down my now splotchy and swollen face.

"You keep forgetting, honey, we are not moving away. You will still get to see everyone around town. This is not goodbye. We are just moving the business in a different direction," he gently reminded me.

We had made the plan three years ago to begin a wholesale tea and coffee business with the hopes I could work more normal hours than the Pink Dogwood Tea Room currently allowed. Waking up at four o'clock in the morning to make freshly baked scones from scratch, my legendary quiche and a varied selection of desserts developed from my grandmother's recipes, had turned me into a sleep deprived zombie. Shane and I had a dream of continuing the tea business and working "smarter not harder." Somehow I thought it would take much longer for the wholesale business to grow.

A large warehouse building and six full-time employees later, Smoky Mountain Coffee, Herb and Tea Company was in full swing. The time to transition had come. It was bitter sweet for me.

How was I going to break the news to everyone that we would be selling the tea room? After all, the Pink Dogwood Tea Room was the central hub for all the ladies who loved to lunch and share afternoon tea. It would be next to impossible to add up all the young girls who had shared their princess teas over the years. We had several Red Hat chapters in our area and surrounding towns who loved to come to the tea room. They were the mainstay of our business. Hopefully, whoever purchased the historic Victorian "Pink Lady" as we referred to her, would love it as much as I did.

"Are you going to let the girls know tonight?" Shane inquired. I was getting ready to drive over to Olivia's ranch for a cookout. I was loading everything up in the car and getting ready to head over. He knew telling them would be the hardest part for me. The tea room was our favorite gathering spot and how we all had first met. Who would have thought sharing a pot of tea could bring such different people close together?

"I really don't want to tell them, but I would hate for them to hear it through the real estate grapevine," I added with dread in my voice. In small southern towns, news travels faster than a bootlegger running moonshine. I could be assured this tidbit of gossip would take off like a rocket.

My friends and I were fondly known about town as "The Traveling Tea Ladies." We earned the nickname from the numerous escapades we'd shared on our travels near and far. We viewed life as one big tea party and managed to have fun and incorporated tea whenever we're together.

We recently returned from a week aboard a tea themed

cruise. Every day we partook of afternoon tea, attended cooking classes featuring tea as an ingredient, participated in educational tea tastings, and learned from leading speakers in the tea industry. We were almost asked to leave the disco when Cassandra had one too many tea-infused vodka "tea-tinis" and began *Dirty Dancing* with the captain while his angry wife watched from her table.

Cassandra Reynolds came from old money, the kind that comes from a third generation candy business old money. Her model-like thin frame and platinum blonde hair drew attention wherever she went. Of course, she always appeared on Dogwood Cove's "Best Dressed List," which is a most coveted title in this little town. And she should! She could always be found in Paris and Milan during Fashion Week as she jetted about with her Hollywood "A List" friends.

Cassandra was just as much at home in her lakeside mansion in Tennessee with her politically connected husband, Doug, as she was in her homes in Sonoma Valley, Palm Beach or her townhouse in Paris. Doug may be the president of the family candy business, but Cassandra was the brains behind its recent success. After all, it was her brilliant idea of using her Hollywood connections to get Reynolds's Candies placed in all the Oscar gift bags, a move that re-launched the candy company's popularity.

Sarah McCaffrey was our local librarian. In comparison to Cassandra, she lived a modest life in a small cottage rental on the outskirts of town. Unlike Cassandra, she wouldn't be caught dead in a hip salon or attending a Hollywood premiere. She preferred her natural brunette hair cropped short and her glasses in "Sally Jesse Raphael" red. Her hard work ethic and creative ideas helped her secure the position of committee chairperson for this year's Dogwood Cove Apple Festival.

Sarah was a quiet, yet quirky addition to the group. Her outlandish outfits inspired by her latest "cause-of-the-day" often left many of our town's residents wondering, *"where DOES she do her shopping?"* The area children adored her and storytelling time at the library was often a standing room only event with Sarah and the toddler set. You could be assured she would wear a flamboyant costume to go along with her literary selection of the day.

Olivia Rivers was the red head in our foursome. Her love of barrel racing and all things related to horseback riding, including the occasional cowboy, resulted in Olivia building her dream, Riverbend Ranch. When most people encountered all five feet of Olivia, they were surprised she could rope a calf and hauled bales of hay better than most farmhands. But one full day of work around Riverbend Ranch and they would know she is all business. Her sometimes brash and sassy attitude kept most people at bay, but anyone who truly knew Olivia would say she has a heart the size of Texas.

And to round out our foursome of The Traveling Tea Ladies was me—Amelia Spencer, local tea expert and owner of the Pink Dogwood Tea Room. My passion for tea began during my college years when I studied abroad in London. The experience inspired me to create a haven for guests to experience authentic afternoon tea. I also enjoyed teaching etiquette lessons, children's cooking classes, and conducted tea tastings.

I'd been married to my husband, Shane, for fifteen years and we had two beautiful children, Emma fourteen and

Charlie twelve. We led a fairly calm life aside from owning two businesses which kept us working much of the time. It had been difficult to juggle Emma's band performances, the kids' nightly homework review and Charlie's football practices and games, but somehow we happily managed.

On first impression, most people would describe me as a down to earth and even tempered person. My wardrobe was rather tailored and classic, very understated in comparison to Sarah's carefree costumes. I usually wore my shoulder length dark blonde hair twisted in a French knot or sleek ponytail to keep the health inspector happy during business hours. Besides tea, my other secret addictions were dark chocolate and my VW bug, nicknamed "Lady Bug" for her red body and black ragtop.

Tonight we were meeting at Riverbend Ranch for Olivia's famous BBQ ribs. Most Tennesseans prefer our sauce on the sweet side with the addition of brown sugar and molasses. Olivia was providing the ribs and the rest of us were bringing the sides.

I was taking my grandmother's antique deviled egg dish filled with our southern staple for summer get-togethers. I made my deviled eggs in the traditional style with a dollop of Dijon mustard, sweet pickle relish, a splash of red wine vinegar and mayonnaise. They were always a hit and I had brought a large plastic container filled with plenty of back-ups. I also had a key lime pie in the cooler along with a gallon of my favorite iced peach tea. That surprise would be for later.

"Hey, Amelia!" Olivia called out as she coughed. The thick smoke from her grill began to get to her. "I didn't hear you drive up."

She was wearing a pair of her favorite Wranglers and a turquoise v-neck blouse. It contrasted beautifully with her red hair. She had on a pair of dangling amber beaded earrings, a feminine touch to this short statured cowgirl.

"Boy those ribs smell amazing," I drooled as I inhaled the savory aromas.

"The ribs are coming along well," Olivia stated wiping the sauce from her hands on a kitchen towel. "What have you been up to today?"

"I've got some news to share with you," I started to tell her.

"Wait a minute, wait a minute," Cassandra called out, her hands full carrying an oversized icy pitcher. "I've brought Lynchburg Lemonade to the party!"

In case you've never tried Lynchburg Lemonade, it is made with Jack Daniels and has a real kick to it. The Tennessee distillery is a short drive from Dogwood Cove and has always been a favorite destination for tourists to our fine Volunteer state. Their "Tipsy Cakes" have been a best seller in the tea room gift shop.

Cassandra set down the pitcher and took a large Louis Vuitton tote bag off her shoulder. She began unwrapping and distributing elegant crystal high balls.

"Here you go, Livy!" she sang as she handed Olivia her lemonade. "Drink up dear and let's get this party started!"

"Nice outfit," smirked Olivia. "How much did your country club getup cost you?" she joked.

"It's *just* Polo," Cassandra whined through her nose as she smoothed her white linen skirt and adjusted her hot pink cardigan tied smartly around her shoulders. "Where did you get your garb? Rodeos-R-Us?" she teased.

"You two should really be nicer to each other," piped up Sarah who was walking up the steps to the bricked patio area. She was costumed in a short denim skirt, light brown suede vest and matching Pocahontas inspired fringed moccasins. She wore her hair in two short braids tied at the ends with feathers.

"I just love the view of the Smoky Mountains from here. I never get tired of them," she sighed.

She was right. The view was exceptional from Olivia's back porch and patio. The whole town was nestled in a valley surrounded by two mountain chains, the Appalachians and the Smokies. The vistas throughout Dogwood Cove were breathtaking. Fall was always spectacular here, but spring was when the tourists would flock to our area to photograph the pink and white blooms of the Dogwood trees. The town's people had planted a large number of trees back in the 1960's in hopes of our area becoming a tourist destination.

"Hey Sarah, what have you brought?" I asked as I jumped up and helped her carry a large tray loaded with covered casserole dishes.

"Oh, just my corn fritters, fried green tomatoes and potato salad," she announced, rather proud of herself.

"You make me look bad, Sarah," Cassandra said as he took another sip of her lemonade. "All I cooked tonight were the cocktails."

Cassandra was a self-proclaimed kitchen screw up. Running a corporation took up most of her time, so she had never fine-tuned her cooking skills. What she did excel in perfecting was having the right contacts. She must have had twelve caterers on speed dial, ready at a moment's notice. It was a well-known fact her last dinner party was prepared by

Oprah's personal chef flown in from Chicago for an intimate party of eight. Our hometown paper, *The Dogwood Daily*, wrote an article covering the exclusive soirée.

"We have plenty, Cassandra!" Olivia yelled over the noise of sizzling ribs. "I have a mess of baked beans and I'm grilling corn on the cob."

Olivia loved taking charge of the grill as much as she loved taking charge of the horses and all the animals at the ranch. It was a big leap for her to purchase the property, but it was a risk she had gladly taken.

Riverbend Ranch was not only a great place to horseback ride along the picturesque Tennessee River, it was also a therapeutic horseback riding center for kids with both physical and developmental challenges. There were only a handful of therapeutic riding centers in the US and Olivia was proud to have nearly fifty students a week riding with a growing wait list. If she could only add more hours to her already long day and add more volunteers, she might be able to accommodate more kids.

Volunteering is how our foursome met. I was hosting an appreciation tea at the Pink Dogwood for community volunteers. Sarah was in attendance for her work at the library and the Apple Festival. Olivia was representing Riverbend Ranch and Cassandra her endowment of the arts. It was an auspicious meeting to say the least. We have been fast friends ever since.

"Let's set your tray over here," I suggested to Sarah. "I don't know how you carried this all by yourself."

She smiled and gave me a quick hug as I set down her contributions and popped a warm corn fritter in my mouth. It was simply wonderful.

"Spit it out, Amelia. What's this big news I interrupted?" Cassandra demanded.

"First, let's toast the evening," I stammered, trying to stall my announcement. Everyone grabbed their lemonade. "To us, 'The Traveling Tea Ladies' and our tea adventures." We nosily clanked our crystal highballs.

Olivia set the ribs in the center of the enormous trestle table flanked with long benches. We sat down and could hear the river churning over the rocks creating soothing music in the background for our enjoyment.

"Do you mind if I dig in while you tell us your news?" Olivia asked as she proceeded to grab a rib before I had a chance to answer her. If there's one thing I know about Olivia, she works up an appetite with her chores. Some of her previous dates had been quickly schooled that she can easily eat them under the table in five seconds flat. It's always been a wonder to me how she can consume so much and still keep her petite figure.

"Go ahead," I conceded after she was already gnawing on a bone. We were all hungry and the fried green tomatoes were particularly tempting tonight. They are a delicacy in our area because their availability is limited to the summer months.

"Sarah, you have outdone yourself," Cassandra purred. "I don't understand why some man hasn't snatched you up by now!" Sarah smiled warmly at the compliment.

"Amelia, out with it," Olivia urged.

"Alright," I paused as I fought back tears.

"What in the world is wrong?" Olivia said alarmed. "Did Shane do something? If he did, I will hogtie him!" She took another rib off the platter and continued eating.

We all remembered the last time one of Olivia's former beaus had been caught necking with an mystery blonde in his pickup truck. Olivia had taken Carrie Underwood's cheating ballad to heart and left a nice indentation in the driver's door.

"Heavens no!" I quickly exclaimed. If there was one person I could count on besides these three friends, it was the steady support of my husband. We had been through many challenges during our marriage and had a rock solid foundation.

"Don't scare us like that," Sarah said breathlessly. "I couldn't handle it if you two broke up. I think I would totally give up on men and relationships all together."

Sarah had just ended a six month relationship with Jake White, reporter for *The Dogwood Daily*. We all thought Jake's creative writing background and high intellect would be a good match. We were not sure what had happened since Sarah was not one to divulge the gory details of their breakup. Who knows? Maybe they would still work it out.

"Ya'll are so funny! It's not anything serious. Shane and I are more than fine," I reassured them.

"You two make me sick," Cassandra spoke up. "I wish Doug still looked at me that way. You guys look like you haven't ended the honeymoon phase yet."

Cassandra and Doug had been married close to ten years. They chose not to have children due to their busy corporate lifestyles. They seemed to have a solid partnership both at home and at Reynolds's Candies.

There were rumors about town that Doug would be calling in favors from their Hollywood "A list" friends if he should decide to run for Senate. Cassandra was tight lipped about his political prospects and I didn't bother to ask. Good friends should know when to respect each other's privacy.

"Get on with the news," Olivia murmured while finishing another rib. "I'm dying to know. Pass those deviled eggs this way, please," she motioned to Sarah.

I paused and took a deep breath before making my announcement. "We're putting the 'Pink Lady' up for sale." All right, it was out and I had said it.

"What? Why? You're not moving are you?" Olivia dropped her rib and began interrogating me.

"No, no, we're not moving," I answered.

"Why are you selling then? I'm confused," Sarah wondered out loud. Her lip had begun to tremble ever so slightly.

"The wholesale business has taken off and Shane needs my help. It was something we've always planned. It just happened much faster than we thought," I informed them.

Can't he hire more help?" Cassandra asked as she poured refills of lemonade. "I know of several qualified people who would be well suited to work at your tea and coffee business."

"Shane and I started Smoky Mountain Coffee, Herb and Tea to eliminate the long hours in the tea room. We're now at the point it's necessary for me to come on board and focus on my passion-the tea!" I explained. "Shane is all about his coffee. We complement each other so well. It's exciting to contemplate this change, but I'll miss the day-to-day activities of the tea room," I conceded with sadness in my voice.

Sarah was dabbing her eyes and turned away to blow her nose. I had no idea she would take the news to heart.

"Sarah, sweetheart," I comforted her by rubbing her arm. "What's wrong? Why are you crying?"

"You don't realize how much coming to the Pink Dogwood has meant to me over the years," she attempted to speak between hiccups. "I feel at peace and centered when I am there. Who is going to give your guests the kind of attention you do?" She was now sobbing.

"Sarah, calm down," Olivia scolded. "Amelia should be the one crying. She has put her heart and soul into her business. I know I am going to miss your grandmother's key lime pie."

"While we had been consoling Sarah, Olivia had polished off her meal. She was ready for dessert. The only thing she loved more than ribs was satisfying her sweet tooth.

"You did bring dessert?" she asked hopefully , glancing in my direction.

"I did more than that. I brought Shane's favorite organic Guatemalan coffee. Would you mind if I stepped inside to brew a fresh pot?"

"I think I'm ready for coffee and pie too," Cassandra added. "My offer still stands if you need extra help at the warehouse."

"Thanks, Cassandra. I'm sure Shane and I will be expanding our staff in no time. I can't believe how fast the company has grown," I remarked and turned to go inside to make the coffee and plate dessert.

I took the pie out of the cooler and sliced four healthy portions. A little dollop of almond cream and a finishing garnish of fresh strawberry on top and I pronounced it perfect. I placed the pie and steaming mugs of coffee on one of Olivia's serving trays and joined the girls on the patio.

Sarah had composed herself by this time. I was surprised she had reacted so strongly to my news. All was forgotten after a few bites of pie. We were soon laughing and cutting up as usual. Sugar can mend all sorts of problems.

"Amelia, how much are you going to ask for the tea room?" Olivia asked in her typical blunt manner. She was not one to mince words.

Cassandra slapped her arm. "You can be so rude! Do you always have to be so direct?"

"I pride myself on being direct," she replied. Her red headed temper was flaring slightly. "I'm a business woman and this is a business decision. If anyone can help Amelia, it would be us," she concluded.

"You're right," I agreed. "I could use some good business advice right now. And no, I don't mind sharing with you how much I am asking for the tea room. I am selling the building and business together. I would be happy to train whoever buys it and I am including my recipes, inventory and website."

"You can ask a good sum with that arrangement," Cassandra agreed shaking her head deep in thought. "I don't think you will have a problem finding a buyer. Have you selected your real estate agent?" She took another sip from her steaming mug of coffee.

"No I haven't but I know who we won't be using. Sally Stokes nearly botched the deal when we were negotiating the purchase of the tea room. That was a nightmare! Plus on a personal note, she's loud-mouthed and drives me insane," I confessed.

"And she's a busy body," Olivia added. "If there's one thing I cannot stand, its people who poke their nose where it doesn't belong." She stood up to get another piece of pie.

"There's much more than just one thing you can't stand

such as men who chew tobacco, people who talk on their cell phones while driving, people who park their shopping carts in the middle of the aisle at the grocery store and block the way of others. Shall I continue?" she winked.

"I admit I have a few pet peeves," Olivia shrugged her shoulders. "I like to think I'm particular." She took a large bite of pie and smiled smugly at Cassandra.

"More like peculiar!" Cassandra shrieked and slapped her knee impressed with her own joke. Don't let these two ladies fool you. Even though they banter back and forth regularly, they are fond of each other. Opposites attract!

"I hate for this evening to come to an end," I yawned and stretched my arms above my head, "but I've got to get an early start in the morning. We're hosting Rebecca Givens princess tea party along with our regular Saturday afternoon tea crowd.

"Need some help?" Sarah offered. "I'm not scheduled to work tomorrow at the library and you know I love children's tea parties." I was glad to see she was smiling again.

"Great! Can you come at ten o'clock? I could use the help setting up for the party," I replied.

Sarah had a way with children, a way with Southern cooking and a way with detailed decorating. She was talented though she did get carried away with her wardrobe at times. For instance, she tried to wear her hair in a bee-hive to complement her 1960's vintage dress she found at "New to You" consignment boutique. Instead of retro, she resembled a crazed fan from a *B-52s* concert. But much like Olivia, she had a heart of gold. Children were her soft spot.

We all helped to clear and wash up the dishes before we packed our gear and went our separate ways. I left Olivia

what was left of the pie and peach iced which she gladly accepted. Tomorrow would hold its own worries and surprises.
What I needed tonight was good sleep.

TWO

"What did the girls think of the big news?" Shane asked bright and early the next morning. He was still in his slippers and bathrobe, but had voluntarily risen to join me on the back porch. It was a ritual of ours to sneak some quality time in before our day got started.

I sipped my tea and sighed as contentment washed over me. "This Darjeeling is some of the best we've tried. What estate did you purchase this from?"

"Amelia, we'll talk tea later. Tell me the details," Shane urged "I bet Cassandra flipped out."

"Actually, it was Sarah who was the most upset." I filled him in on the details of my visit with the girls last night.

"It was nice of Sarah to help you today. There's no telling how many extra reservations you will have," Shane mused.

"You're right," I groaned. Saturday mornings were always a scramble. No matter how many scones I baked, there never seemed to be enough. I learned to make them ahead and freeze them so I could pop them in the oven for last minute guests.

"I've got to run," I said as I gave Shane a quick kiss good-bye. "Let's plan on seven for dinner tonight. I've got the pot roast in the crock pot. And remind Emma that Julia's Mom is picking her up at one o'clock for the movies."

"Anything else?" he teased. He playfully swatted my fanny as I passed him.

"Yes, as a matter-of-fact, Charlie has football practice at two o'clock. Call me if you need me," I waved over my shoulder.

I fired up "Lady Bug" and headed south for the five mile drive to work. It was only six o'clock, but I could already feel the humidity in the air. I played Journey on the CD player and sang along. Gosh, no one could sing like Steve Perry anymore.

I was sufficiently ready to tackle whatever the day held. As I entered the back door to the kitchen, I turned the A/C on high and checked the voicemail. Good, not too many messages, only five; five more guests attending the Givens Princess Party, Mrs. Roberts wanted her favorite table overlooking the herb garden for afternoon tea today, and two more reservations for our "Tea by the Sea" next weekend.

Drat, a message from Sally Stokes! I inwardly groaned as I listened to her three minute message. She said she would be dropping by sometime today, exactly what I didn't want to hear.

People often have the misconception that tea room owners have all the time in the world to join their guests for a pot of tea. A successful owner creates an atmosphere and ambiance that makes everyone feel relaxed and comfortable. No one truly realizes all the work behind the scenes in crafting this experience. Today would be one of those days when I would be too rushed to deal with Sally Stokes. I reminded myself to tell the servers I would be busy in the kitchen if she came by unannounced.

Today would be hectic with the Givens Princess Party for twenty-five guests along with our afternoon tea reservations at two and four o'clock. There would be an additional thirty-five patrons sipping and savoring. I was glad to have Sarah helping.

I quickly washed my hands, slipped on my burgundy and toile apron and began preparations for a quadruple bath of chocolate chip scones, a special request from the birthday girl.

I viewed this quiet time of the morning when the rest of the world was asleep as my personal meditation. Baking and cooking have always been therapeutic for me and as the music of my favorite Yo Yo Ma CD filled the kitchen, I felt all the worries of yesterday lift from my shoulders.

As I gently rolled out the dough, I caught a glimpse of a bright red cardinal from the kitchen window. He was sitting on the fence sharing his morning song. He was a regular at the bird feeder and I enjoyed the tenderness he displayed towards his mate.

Adding the herb garden and birdfeeders provided an ever-changing view. Shane and Charlie had worked together to clear the space and get the flower beds ready. The addition of the birdhouses was a Mother's Day present from the children. The thought of leaving them behind made my heart ache. We would have to recreate this beautiful herb garden and bird haven outside my new office window.

The phone rang shrilly and jolted me from my daydreaming. Who was calling at six thirty in the morning? I wiped the dough remnants from my hands and grabbed the it on the third ring.

"Good Morning. Thanks for calling the Pink Dogwood Tea Room," I cheerfully said. "How can I help you?"

"Hey, Amelia, it's Lacy," a sleepy voice said. "I'm feeling horrible this morning. I don't think I will be able to make it today."

Lacey was a college student who most likely had been out late again. This was the third time in a month she called in sick on a Saturday. Illness was understandable and no one should work when they were sick. But, three times in a month and on our busiest day of the week? I wasn't buying it.

"Gee, Lacey, again?" I asked sarcastically. If there's one thing I can't, stand, it is irresponsible behavior. Our guests tipped generously and the servers were well compensated. I couldn't understand her apathetic attitude.

"This has become quite a habit with you. Maybe it's time you thought of moving on if your schedule at the tea room is interfering with your extracurricular activities," I suggested. There, I had said it and I felt better getting it off my chest. She didn't appreciate her job and I had let it continue for too long.

I think my comment must have caught Lacy off-guard. She didn't have a quick response. "In fact ,Lacey, there are going to be some changes around here, so maybe this is for the best," I informed her.

"I'm sorry, Amelia. I let you down again. You're right; I think I should move on." She didn't seem especially devastated. If anything, she sounded relieved.

"I appreciate your honesty but I need people I can count on. I wish you all the best and I will call you when the accountant has your final paycheck ready," I said as my voice softened. Having these talks was a necessary part of business. In my heart, I knew this was a good decision.

"OK, Amelia. Sorry," she said and hung up. That was that. No time to cry over spilled milk, I reasoned with myself.

Back to my bird show and an hour later, scones were baked, cream of tomato soup was simmering, and sixty beautiful mini artichoke quiches were ready for the oven. Everything was on schedule and my frustration with Lacey long forgotten.

Sarah was due to come in soon along with Emily and Gretchen who had worked at the Pink Dogwood since our opening. What was nice about these two ladies was they automatically knew what to do without me asking. They refilled the sugar cube bowls. If any of our sixty teas were low, they filled out a low inventory alert form to be faxed over to Shane. They stocked the beverage station, sliced lemons, filled creamers with milk, and did it all with a smile. It was like a tight run ship. Any detail that could be done ahead saved time and allowed attention to be on the guests.

"Good morning!" Sarah chirped as she came in. She hung her purse on the coat rack and looked for a freshly pressed apron.

"Good morning. I'm so glad you are here," I told her as Emily and Gretchen arrived right behind her. I was working on configuring the seating diagram and warned them it would be a 'dilly of a day.' The four of us descended on the dining rooms and began placing the teacups, saucers, and place settings on the tables.

I never tire of admiring our beautiful Victorian home from the sweeping curved staircase to the ornate wallpaper in the foyer. She was stunning; the original hardwood floors, tiffany stained glass chandeliers, tiled fireplaces and twelve foot ceilings caught the attention of many admirers.

My favorite space in the house was the downstairs powder room decorated with five different wallpaper treatments, including the ceiling. The piece de la resistance was the original claw foot tub. I could imagine the mistress of the house spending hour upon hour soaking in a hot bubble bath in this luxurious space.

Our smaller, more intimate dining room was originally the parlor now decorated in soft hues of blue and pink. The stained-glass mantle bore a tulip and heart motif. Muted patterns of birds and roses adorned the wallpaper. We could accommodate twelve around the antique tables. It was the perfect spot to visit with friends and create a special memory.

The gift shop was located past the foyer and served as the first owner's dining room. The center piece of this gorgeous room was the cobalt blue tiled fireplace with matching fireplace insert. The walls are lined with our entire assortment of teas, hand poured candles, gift baskets, teapots and coffees along with Shane's antiques.

As we placed the last of the cups and saucers on the tables, the front door opened and our first appointments arrived. Sarah would act as greeter and take each diner to their table. Gretchen and Emily had their table and party assignments. Everyone worked together like clockwork. I was free to head to the kitchen.

After each guest had selected their choice of hot tea, they would be presented soup for their first course. The second course was scones served with almond cream, strawberry preserves, and homemade lemon curd.

The British style three tiered tray was the grand finale. The individual quiches, cucumber and herb cream cheese tea sandwiches, and mini turkey and cranberry grilled Paninis made up the savory layer. The dessert tier was a hit! Key lime truffles rolled in toasted coconut, chocolate dipped strawberries and miniature chocolate bliss Bundt cakes comprised this sweet layer. We always served one large dessert and today's selection was a triple berry English trifle with lemon sponge cake. It was worth every decadent calorie.

Sarah and Emily handled the Givens party with ease. I managed to step out of the kitchen and visit the dining rooms. It was sweet seeing all the princesses in attendance this morning. The girls were adorable in their tiaras and dress up gowns. These were enjoyable parties to host. A quick tidying of pink boa feathers and a few stray sequins and we were ready for the two o'clock afternoon tea crowd.

The ladies drifted in slowly. Some perused the gift shop for treasures while they waited to be seated. Sales of our newest tea selection, peppermint patty, kept Gretchen busy at the cash register. The aroma of fresh peppermint with dark chocolate wafted from the kitchen.

"Things are going well," Sarah smiled as she breezed through the kitchen door way. "We've had to make several pitchers of your peach iced tea with this heat wave."

"Thanks for coming today, Sarah," I spoke sincerely. I told her about the phone call from Lacey earlier this morning and she shook her head sadly.

"If I had a job like this, you couldn't keep me away. I love working at the library and spending time with the children. The downside is we are open seven days a week and also in the evenings. Sometimes I wish I could set my own schedule like you do," she confided to me.

"You definitely set your own schedule when you run a tea room," I laughed and took a seat on a nearby stool. My feet were aching already. "It's usually much longer hours than a regular job. Emma complains if she wants to spend time with me, she has to come here. But there are wonderful fringe benefits for her such as inviting her friends to a private tea party and always having a fresh baked treat to enjoy afterschool," I elaborated.

"My idea of a childhood dream come true," Sarah sighed wistfully.

"Would you be interested in filling in again when your schedule allows?" I asked hopefully. Sarah had done an outstanding job with the princess party and more than one mother had been overheard singing her praises about her patience and kindness with the girls. She paused and set her tray on the counter. I recognized she was deep in thought when she began twirling her brunette hair.

"I want to talk with you and Shane about something," she began when we were suddenly interrupted by Sally Stokes' rude arrival.

"Hello, hello, ladies and Miss Amelia!" Sally said waving her hands in the air resembling a flapping bird's wings. "How are y'all doing this beautiful day?"

How had she managed to get past my pit bulls, I wondered? And she had chosen to ignore the sign posted at the entrance to the kitchen that plainly stated "Employees Only." Rules were for everyone else but Sally Stokes, I thought amusing myself.

"Hey, Sally. I got your message and unfortunately, we are very busy today. We're in the middle of our afternoon tea reservations. Can I call you later when it's a better time?" I asked civilly.

"This won't take long, 'pinky promise,'" she sang out in

a shrill, high pitched twang extending her pinky finger in the air.

She was going to be harder to get rid of than bed bugs! Boy this woman wouldn't take no for an answer.

"What can I do for you?" I said impatiently.

"I heard from a certain someone that y'all are selling the Pink Dogwood!" she exclaimed and put her hands on ample hips before continuing. "And I said, 'Well no one told me!' So here I am, ready with paperwork to list this house." She took out a thick packet of papers from her tote bag and slapped them down on the counter. "When do you want to schedule your open house? Is next weekend a good time? It doesn't leave much time to run an ad in the paper, but if I call this afternoon, we can make the deadline." She grinned with a saccharin smile oblivious to anyone and everything going on around her.

"No, next week is not a good time," I informed her. "Who told you we were selling the tea room?" I asked as I approached her.

"Oh, I'll never tell. A little birdie whispered in my ear," she pantomimed as she began to giggle, her body shaking like jelly.

I was getting hot under the collar. Sally was putting me on the spot and my laid-back personality was being tested.

Sarah quickly exited the kitchen taking care of the guests who were ready to be seated for afternoon tea. We would have to continue our conversation later.

"Sally, you'll have to forgive me but I have to put together tea trays and as I explained earlier, this is not a good time," I said feeling my face start to flush. I hoped she took the hint and high-tailed it out of here.

"That's OK, sugar. I can wait back here in the kitchen and have a tall glass of your peach iced tea. I'll wait until you're finished and then we can discuss details," she insisted plopping herself down on the bar stool.

"Oh, no!" I cried out emphatically. "We will be here for hours. Besides, I will have to talk to Shane before I fill out any paperwork."

"Oh," she straightened up and began gathering her things. "You have one of those dictatorship marriages. You have to run everything by the 'man of the house,' right?" she asked playing devil's advocate while watching me from the corner of her eye.

This overbearing woman was pushing it!

"Sarah, would you help Ms. Stokes out?" I yelled with forced happiness in my voice into the gift shop. I turned towards Sally with a plastered Cheshire grin on my face.

"It's been real nice, Amelia," she murmured as she sashayed out the kitchen doorway. "Call me!" she called out over her shoulder.

It would be a cold day in H-E-Double L hockey sticks, I thought to myself. I was going to ask Shane *who* leaked this information and then promptly hang them by their toenails!

THREE

I picked up Emma and Julia at the mall and directed "Lady Bug" home. I wanted to speak to Shane to find out how Sally had heard our news so quickly.

"Mom, you just ran a red light!" Emma squealed from the back seat. "Are you feeling all right?" Her big blue eyes were as large as saucers as I looked at her in the rearview mirror.

"Oh my word! All I need right now is a ticket," I exclaimed as I slowed down below the speed limit. "I'm sorry girls. I seem to be distracted this afternoon."

I continued my much slower pace and focused on getting home safely without a run in with the law. Today I was lucky.

"My Mom does that too, Mrs. Spencer. No worries," Julia spoke up. I think she was relieved we were in her driveway safe and sound.

A few short blocks down the road and we were pulling into our own garage. Shane stood by the door with a mud covered Charlie.

"Hey Mom, I threw three touchdowns," he informed us. Sweat streamed down his dirt streaked face. I noticed his once round face was now thinning and his shoulders were becoming broader. He was transitioning from a little boy into a young man right before my eyes.

"Excellent, Charlie. I can't wait to see your first game. This is going to be your year, I can feel it!" I said proudly.

Shane tousled Charlie's hair and patted his back, beaming with pride. He was Shane made over complete with freckles across the bridge of his nose.

"Hey bud. Why don't you head to the shower while I get dinner ready," I suggested to Charlie. "And don't forget to scrub behind your ears this time," I called out as he quickly ran inside.

"Emma, could you help set the table while I speak to Dad in private?"

"Sure Mom," she replied and stepped inside closing the door. She was turning out to be such a responsible young lady. I was amazed that so far I had been able to enjoy the teen years.

Shane turned towards me with concern on his face. "What's wrong? Did something happen at work today?"

"I guess you could say that," I told him. "Let's head to the porch and I'll fill you in."

I walked through our cozy kitchen and inhaled the aroma of pot roast wafting throughout the house. I grabbed the stack of today's mail and carried it outside with me. I plopped down in my favorite wicker chair and took a sideways glance at Shane. I loved sitting on the porch this time of day when the temperatures cooled down. It was a wonderful extension of our living space and had become a haven to share our most important news and decision making.

"Enough suspense already! What's going on?" he asked taking a seat next to me.

"Did you call Sally Stokes and tell her we were selling?" I asked locking eyes with him. I shared with him Sally's surprise visit to the kitchen and retold my conversation with her. He seemed shocked.

"Why would I do that after the stress she caused us before? Honestly, I don't know how she found out. I do have some news to tell you, though," he said solemnly and paused. "I have a buyer."

"A buyer? For what? For the tea room?" My head felt like it was spinning. I hardly had time to process the fact we were selling. Now he had a buyer!

"Dawson Interiors wants to buy the building. They want to open a new location in Dogwood Cove," he divulged.

"Dawson Interiors from Nashville?" I recalled. Jake White had done a nice write up in *The Dogwood Daily* when the firm had sponsored a room in the Symphony Showcase house. Cassandra was good friends with several of the designers.

"Yes. They approached me a few months ago and asked if we were interested in selling," he reported.

"Why didn't you mention this to me then?" I asked straightening in my chair.

"It didn't seem like the right time to sell, so I didn't bother telling you," he replied.

"Didn't bother telling me? How could you decide not to share something so important regarding our business?" I asked perplexed. I trusted Shane with most business decision, so this revelation surprised me.

"You were in the middle of your *Southern Living Magazine* photo shoot. Remember how you were barely sleeping because you were worried about all the details?" he gently reminded me. "I didn't want to add to your stress level when it was obviously not the time to consider selling."

I recalled that week and how I had been a nervous wreck. I had cleaned like a fiend every inch of the tea room, practiced my recipes repeatedly and perfected the food presentation for the photographer. The extra gardening time alone would have driven anyone mad. The article had turned out well and resulted in a beautiful story about tourism in Dogwood Cove. It had been worth the extra effort.

"Yes, that was a very stressful time," I admitted shaking my head. "No wonder you didn't tell me. I hardly ate that week and was on the verge of a meltdown."

"Dawson Interiors had made a substantial offer and one we would be foolish to turn down in this economy. It's three times what we paid for the property," he disclosed.

"Three times?" I asked in shock. "That's wonderful. I never thought to expect that much. Are they planning on running the Pink Dogwood Tea Room downstairs and housing their offices upstairs?"

Shane's face said it all. I didn't want to hear what he had to say next. "No, sweetie, there will not be a tea room. The entire house will be for their showroom and offices," he informed me with sadness in his voice.

I sat back and my mouth fell open. I didn't know what to say, what to think and suddenly the realization hit me. No tea room. No princess parties. No tea tastings. No special venue to celebrate life's important milestones such as baby showers and bridal tea parties. This was a blow. I felt as though I were losing a best friend.

"I don't know about this, Shane. I don't feel good about this decision," I admitted and shook my head. "This is going to be devastating for so many of the ladies in town. When we talked about selling, we talked about continuing the business and training the new owners. I assumed the Pink Dogwood would remain open," I concluded as my voice quivered and hot tears burned my eyes. Shane knew how much the tea room meant to me. I had put my heart, soul, and sweat equity into building the business and had developed a loyal following.

"Amelia, I know you are upset, but I don't think we should pass up this offer," he soothed me as he dabbed my eyes with a tissue. "This is a substantial offer. Think of how far ahead we will be. Don't forget you will be busy with Smoky Mountain Coffee, Herb and Tea."

Yeah, he had resigned himself to the sale and had moved on. He was far more practical than I and viewed business as business. I, on the other hand, was more emotional. I couldn't imagine the tea room closing.

I glanced down at my lap and the forgotten mail now covered with splattered tears. There was an envelope on top with a running mustang logo. I assumed another college fundraiser needed my attention. I tore into the mail, glad to have a distraction at the moment. I opened the letter from my Alma Mater, Southern Methodist University, a small liberal arts college of about six thousand undergraduates nestled in the Highland Park area of Dallas.

"What's that?" Shane inquired.

"As if my day couldn't get any better, I just received a reminder that I am getting older. Check for grey hair," I sighed. "It's an invitation to homecoming and my twenty-year college reunion."

"Old SMU," Shane mused. "Sounds like fun!"

I had taken the family for a weekend visit several years ago. The campus was gorgeous. The Georgian style architecture, bricked walkways and immaculate landscaping gave the school an Ivy League feel. I could still remember my first visit when I was eighteen, back when I sported an 80's permed poof. During the tour I was overwhelmed by the impressive buildings, fountains, and Dallas Hall. It seemed so long ago and I didn't want to be reminded that so much time had passed.

"I think I will put this invitation in the shredder," I said getting up from the chair.

"Hold on, Amelia. I think it would be good to have a change of scenery with all the transitions going on. A weekend on campus sounds good to me," he smiled brightly oblivious to my darkening mood.

"I am not sure I share your sentiments right now. In fact, I would like to eat dinner and go soak in the tub to clear my head," I said heavy hearted.

He knew a long soak in the tub would change my mood. We could discuss business and reunions another time. A couple scoops of green tea soaking salts and all my troubles would be forgotten. Light a candle; grab a book; and inhale the chamomile, lavender, and peppermint scented bath salt and I would be relaxed. It was what I needed.

"Why don't you run the water and I will make sure the kids eat dinner. You need some time to yourself," he suggested.

I love my husband. He is a mind reader. He knew I needed my space and time to unwind. I decided to take him up on his generous offer.

"You just reminded me again of why you are the world's greatest husband," I grinned and kissed him.

"I plan on collecting from you later," he teased and lifted

his eyebrow. Yes, one date with Shane and I had known he was the one. He understood me better than anyone else.

I ran upstairs to start the bath water. Five minutes later, I could already feel the tension lifting. Thirty minutes later and the stress in my neck and shoulders erased. I put on my favorite fuzzy slippers and robe to join my family downstairs.

Shane was finishing up the dinner dishes and had the dish towel draped over his shoulder. He placed a salad dressed in balsamic vinaigrette in front of me. "There's plenty of pot roast left," he informed me.

"Hello?" I heard from the foyer. "Anyone home?"

"Cassandra? Is that you?" I called out.

"Yes, darlin' it's moi!" she sang out as she slid into the kitchen. "Sit down. Don't let me interrupt your dinner."

"I called Cassandra while you were in the tub and told her to come over," Shane informed me. "Can I get you anything to eat? Something to drink?" he asked my pencil-thin friend.

"Oh, I'm fine unless you have some of Amelia's peach iced tea already made," she requested.

"Coming right up," he said and began filling a glass with ice. He looked over at me to gauge my mood.

"What's going on?" I asked wondering why Shane had called her and what these two had up their sleeves.

"Don't be upset with Shane, Amelia," she said patting my arm. "He told me you had a hard day and thought you were in need of some cheering up. So here I am!"

Cassandra had a way of making everyone around her smile with her magnetic personality. She was a huge flirt and loved to tease. It was hard to stay down with her around. She was very generous with her time and had been a good friend to me over the years.

I took a bite of pot roast and began smiling. "You are a sight for sore eyes. I've really had a trying day." I shared with her Sally's visit to the tea room, the offer from Dawson's Interiors and the class reunion invitation.

"Southern Methodist University was your college?" she recalled.

"Go Mustangs!" Shane cheered as he brought piping hot rolls and butter to the table. Cassandra helped herself and slathered on a pat of butter.

"Sounds like a plan," she said wiping her fingers on her napkin.

"What plan?" I asked confused.

"I have a friend who owns the Adolphus Hotel in downtown Dallas. I'm sure we could book a suite and have a girls' weekend. What do you think? She inquired as she finished her roll.

"Sounds crazy. You're just as bad as he is," I declared and glared in Shane's direction. "The last thing I need right now is a trip down memory lane. There are some things best left in the past."

Shane turned away from the sink and faced me. "Are you talking about your old boyfriend, Jett Rollins?" Shane asked. Did I detect a hint of jealousy in his voice?

"Heavens, no!" I reassured him. "I haven't heard from Jett since his wedding invitation ten years ago."

Jett had been my college boyfriend and for a brief period, we were engaged. Leaving for London my senior year was perfect timing. I immersed myself in the culture, intensely studied, and traveled all over Europe. As soon as I returned to the US, I graduated and moved back to Dogwood Cove. I wondered why he had bothered sending a wedding invitation with the way things were left between us.

"I was thinking more about Katherine," I revealed.

"Have I missed something here?" Cassandra asked. "Who is this Katherine person?" She took a quick sip of her tea and set her glass down, giving me her full attention.

"I loved SMU. I loved going away to college. I loved Dallas. I happened to get placed with a roommate who didn't work out so well," I revealed.

That was the understatement of the century. Katherine and I were polar opposites. She was from the big city—Houston. She was fashion forward and very sexy, which made her popular with the guys on campus. She was a theatre major with a booming voice and a presence about her that made her the center of attention. Her Giorgio Armani Red Door perfume enveloped everything and everyone in its path.

I was very different from Katherine. I had small-town values, dressed modestly, and tended to be on the shy side. I trusted people, maybe a bit too much, and I learned valuable life lessons in the process. I left Dogwood Cove a naïve girl. Katherine had sensed that about me and had taken advantage of it.

"Katherine Gold will probably not make it to the reunion," Shane told me. Did he actually think she would miss an opportunity to be the center of attention?

"Shane, she was our homecoming queen. Former homecoming queens always come back to be presented at halftime," I reminded him.

"This isn't the same Katherine Gold from TV? Which soap opera is she on?" Cassandra tried to recall snapping her fingers. "Didn't she get voted best body in *People Magazine* last year?"

"Yep, that Katherine Gold." I pushed my plate away, suddenly losing my appetite.

"I didn't realize you two were roommates! Why didn't you tell me?" she asked excitedly.

"I wouldn't put it on my top ten list of things people should know about me. I've tried to forget about those years," I sadly told her. I looked over at Shane and saw the look of support in his eyes. He and I had started dating shortly after I returned from SMU. He understood my lack of desire in discussing Katherine.

"I think Amelia is hesitant to talk much about it because rooming with Katherine ended up being a nightmarish situation for her," Shane told Cassandra. "She is nothing like the character she plays on TV."

Many people assumed Katherine was just like her character, Lindsey Tanner, on the long running soap opera, 'The Rich and The Lost.' Lindsey was adored by everyone and exhibited kindness, love, humility, and loyalty, a strict departure from her real life personality.

"So, Katherine Gold is actually a witch," Cassandra guessed. "I've heard a few stories about her in LA, but I've never listened to half the things people gossip about," she stated. Cassandra should know with her "A List" friends. She heard and saw firsthand how different life was in Hollywood.

"I don't like labeling people, so I will not call her a witch," I claimed.

"She was an absolute witch to you and I don't mind being the one to say it," Shane opined.

"I still think Dallas would be a perfect girls' getaway and what better excuse than a homecoming weekend?" Cassandra said in a spirited voice. "I doubt we will even run into this Katherine Gold woman. Don't let her keep you from going. She'll probably be busy getting a mini facelift or tummy tuck," she joked.

"Cassandra has a point, Amelia," Shane agreed. "You could use a fun weekend with the girls. I can hold down the fort and take the kids camping. They would love it." He never ceased to surprise me. He was continually my rock.

"Let me think about it. I'm going to have a lot on my plate with packing up the tea room, scheduling movers, and of course, I will want to hold one final tea party before we close," I thought aloud.

"When's the reunion?" Cassandra interrupted.

"It's five weeks from today. It's the big Rice game," I shared. Rice had been one of our big rivals when SMU had played in the now defunct Southwest Conference. We had played our games at Texas Stadium, which had been a good forty-five minute drive from campus. It was hard to believe it had been torn down and replaced with a new stadium for the Dallas Cowboys.

Now the games were held on campus at the new Gerald J. Ford Stadium completed in 2000. Some of SMU's more famous Alumni included golfer Payne Stewart, First Lady Laura Bush, actor Kathy Bates, Heisman Trophy Winner Doak Walker, and legendary TV producer Aaron Spelling. SMU had quite a history of producing award winning scholars and athletes.

I had not been back for a football game since my freshman year when our football program received the death penalty for recruiting violations, a devastating blow that years later continued to plague the college. We went from posh games at Texas Stadium to no games, no practices, and no recruiting for three years. The new football recruits would have to pass the same stringent enrollment qualifications that every other student had to go through to be accepted at SMU.

I had to admit, I was excited to attend a game at the new stadium. It would be nice to be involved in the homecoming festivities and to see the campus draped in the school colors, red and blue.

"I will let Albert know to reserve the jet and I'll book the suite at the Adolphus," Cassandra said shooting Shane a conspirator's victory smile. "Be prepared to shop because Neiman Marcus is right down the street from the hotel."

Now this was sounding good! I couldn't remember the last time I had stepped foot inside a Neiman Marcus, but I always enjoyed the fantastic store displays Neiman's was known for.

"I will consent to the trip if you will allow me to take everyone to afternoon tea at the French Room at the Adolphus, my treat," I bartered.

"You're on," she crowed. I could feel all the stress from talking about Katherine dissipating. I was beginning to look forward to our weekend in Dallas.

FOUR

The next few weeks flew by at a record pace. With the start of a new school year and preparing for the sale of the tea room, it seemed like every moment of the day was filled.

Shane met with Dawson Interiors and began the real estate contract process. If everything went according to plan, the tea room would be sold the week after we returned from Dallas. I decided to keep the Pink Dogwood open until the last possible day.

As word spread throughout Dogwood Cove about the sale, reservations began pouring in from everywhere. Guests wanted to make sure they had an opportunity to have one last afternoon tea and I was committed to making sure their tea trays were spectacular.

Being so busy kept me from having crying spells. I came close a few times when our "regulars" began pulling out tissues and remarking how saddened they were to no longer have a wonderful place to celebrate special occasions. I agreed but pushed on and reminded myself this was what we had planned from the beginning and tried my best to focus on the bigger picture.

Emma and Charlie had mixed feelings regarding the sale. Now we would have weekends free for family activities.

On the other hand, they had grown up in the tea room and participated in our children's cooking lessons and etiquette classes. They seemed to focus regret on missing the home-made desserts. I reminded them they would still have their goodies, but they would enjoy them at home.

Sarah was instrumental during the transition. She worked with me whenever she had a free day from the library. I was glad to have her assistance with all the added reservations.

"Gosh, I am going to miss being here," she revealed one afternoon. "What are you going to do about Lily? Will she be moving out to your house?" I hated to admit it, but I had not even thought about the cat. She enjoyed lazing on the porch watching the bird show.

Lily had adopted us when she was only three weeks old. I was baking a batch of scones when I heard a terrible commotion coming from next door. I decided to investigate and found a tiny kitten hissing at two large fenced-in dogs. I scooped her up, still spitting and tail puffed, and brought her to our back porch for nourishment. She had been with us ever since.

Her amber eyes and beautiful coloring made her a popular attraction. Whether she was chasing snowflakes or fighting snakes in our herb garden, she kept everyone seated by the windows entertained. Sarah had brought up an important issue—would Lily be happy leaving her porch?

"Have you finished packing for 'Big D?'" I asked her while we were setting tables. We were due to fly out in two days.

"I'm not sure what to pack. I know there will be a cocktail reception Friday evening, then the homecoming game and BBQ Saturday. Am I forgetting anything?"

"Don't forget comfortable shoes for shopping at North Park Mall," I reminded her. "And we might go to Fort Worth for some line dancing. Olivia will be overjoyed to mingle with real cowboys," I laughed.

"Then I'll pack my ostrich boots. I have the perfect outfit for some *'boot scootin' boogie!'*" she giggled as she placed the silverware at each place setting.

I didn't know how we were going to accomplish so many activities into this short trip, but we always managed. This time would be no exception for "The Traveling Tea Ladies."

"I'm glad the library agreed to give you some time off."

"I have seniority since I have worked there for over ten years," she said with a wistful look in her eyes.

Lately, Sarah had seemed much more contemplative than usual. I noticed the change in her since we had been spending more time together

"Sarah, are you feeling all right these days?" I asked her, the concern evident in my voice. "You seem to have something heavy on your mind."

She stepped back and crossed her arms. She appeared to be surprised.

"I'm fine. I have been doing a lot of thinking about life," she admitted.

"Is this about Jake?" I guessed.

"He's part of it. We've been talking recently, but for now, we're keeping it strictly platonic. Actually, the problem is me. I feel so restless. I don't feel like I am doing anything meaningful at the library," she divulged.

This wasn't what I had expected to hear from her. She had been working at the Dogwood Cove Public Library since she was a high school volunteer. She had attended the

University of Tennessee, earned her undergraduate degree and applied for the children's librarian position.

"Are you waiting on a promotion or a raise?" I wondered. I had not heard her mention either, but it was a shot in the dark.

"No, it's not about a promotion or a raise," she said shrugging her shoulders. "I need more!" she exclaimed in earnest.

Sarah was creatively challenged. She yearned to express herself. Her wardrobe was evidence of that. I was sure she had packed whimsical outfits for this weekend. Feeling stifled and underutilized seemed to be what she was battling.

"Don't get me wrong, Amelia," she pleaded. "I love the children and people I work with. It's all I have been doing for ten years and I need a change. I don't know how else to explain it," she said exasperated.

I understood how she felt. I had taken a risk when I left my steady paycheck to open the tea room.

"I do understand what you mean," I reassured her and gave her a hug. "I have actually been in your shoes. Change can be exciting!"

"I'm hoping to figure some of this out while we are in Dallas," she said with a hopeful smile.

"You've been a good friend to me over the years, Sarah. If I can be of help, I am here for you."

"Thanks, Amelia," she brightened. "Working with you on and off the past few weeks has been fun. I feel as though I've been able to see the other side of running running a business and I have enjoyed it," Sarah smiled and squeezed my hand.

"Hey, let's make a pot of tea and sit down. Which tea

would you like to try today; jasmine, apricot or genmaicha? You decide."

"I would like to try the Japanese genmaicha. The aroma reminds me of a rice cake. All the polyphenols and antioxidants have convinced me to drink at least four cups a day to keep me healthy."

"I think this tea is so interesting with the kernels of fried rice that puff up like miniature popcorn. It's a best seller with our customers," I informed her.

"I can see why," she said as she inhaled the aroma of the steeping tea. "I can't wait to try it," she announced as she brought the cup up to her lips.

And she wasn't disappointed. It was the perfect pot of tea for two friends sharing their dreams, their aspirations, and their hopes for the future.

"We need to do this more often," I told her. "Sometimes it's hard for me to stop and take time to do even something as simple as have a cup of tea. Maybe I will be forced to do that more often since I will have to do taste testing and blending—one of the perks of the business!"

"What about your tea tasting classes? Are you still going to teach those?" Sarah inquired.

"I haven't figured that out yet, but I still would like to have classes on a regular basis. That would allow me to keep in touch with many of our guests. I will have to start looking for a venue to host the tastings," I shared with her.

We finished our tea and exchanged goodbyes. I had a long list of errands to run not to mention I had to finish packing.

My first stop was to get Emma from Riverbend Ranch. She was volunteering today with the therapeutic riding classes.

Olivia was unloading a truck full of hay. She was swinging bales from the back of the flatbed into the hay loft where one of the farmhands was waiting to stack them. She handled the heavy bales as if they were as light as a bag full of cotton. She never ceased to amaze me.

"Hey there, Amelia!" she called to me, wiping sweat from her brow with her forearm. "It sure is a hot one today!"

Even though it was October, the days were still quite warm. I loved the crisp fall mornings in Dogwood Cove and the brilliant sapphire blue autumnal skies. It was my favorite time of year.

"If you think it's hot here, wait until we get to Dallas. I hope you packed light weight clothes for the trip," I advised her.

"I haven't even packed yet. I'm just going to throw a couple of outfits together," Olivia admitted.

That was typical of Olivia. Carefree, not concerned with fashion. She would pack her favorite jeans and something comfortable. She always managed to look beautiful no matter what she wore.

"Liv, you're forgetting the cocktail party. Do you have a black dress?" I suggested.

"I was thinking more of a dressy pant suit. Don't worry, I won't let you down," she assured me.

I should have guessed pant suit. She would look fantastic.

"Carl, I'm taking a break for a minute," she called up to the hayloft. "Let's have something cold to drink and go inside for a minute," she said to me.

"Good idea, Liv."

I loved her kitchen with its arched stone fireplace and antique farmhouse table. It was a cozy addition to the house and the perfect place to share conversation while looking out at the river rushing below.

"What can I get you to drink? A soft drink, water, or lemonade iced tea?"

"The lemonade iced tea sounds perfect. Thanks!" And it was perfect. Cold, slightly sweet and tart, all at the same time.

"Cassandra told me about this Katherine Gold woman. Amelia, what's the story on her?"

I cleared my throat and paused a moment. I took another sip of tea before I began speaking. "Remember I dated someone at SMU?" I reminded her, not sure of what to say next.

"Dated? I thought you were engaged. What was his name? Jeff? Jed? Judd?"

"Jett. Jett Rollins," I replied flatly. This was becoming hard for me to share.

"I guess everyone was surprised when you came home after graduation. I guess it worked out for the best since you met Shane right after that," Olivia surmised.

Thank the Lord for blessings! Little did I know I was being led to my soulmate. Things happen for a reason.

"Yes, Jett and I were engaged ... briefly, very briefly," I added.

"What was that all about" Olivia asked point blank as she refilled our iced tea glasses.

"Let's say I found him in a compromising situation with another woman," I said as I took a deep breath. "It was my roommate Katherine Gold."

"She IS a witch! I tell you what I would have done. I would have taken her by her goldilocks and tossed her out the door!" Olivia shouted with emphasis and made quick repetitive circles above her head as if she were spinning an invisible lasso. That was Olivia. She was brutally honest and easily hurt.

I started laughing at the visual image of Katherine being hurled around by her hair. At the time that might have been a knee jerk reaction, but I didn't go there. I was never one to get into the gutter to fight. Some may see this as a weakness but I view it as not compromising my values.

"What did you do?"

"I simply walked out the door and never spoke to either one of them again. I was due to fly out the next morning to London." That had been one of the most painful days of my life. I tried hard to block it from my memory and now this class reunion was dredging all those hurt feelings back up.

With time the pain had gradually subsided. After London, I returned home to Dogwood Cove and got busy. Shane had returned home from his summer abroad in Europe backpacking and staying at youth hostels. He happened to be in town visiting his Aunt Alice. We ran into each other at a downtown Friday night music festival and soon became inseparable.

The one thing he had to be patient with me about was trust. After what Jett and Katherine had done, it was going to take me a while. He had graduate school to get back to, so we began a long distance courtship. When I shared what had happened with him, he became angry.

"Why would anyone in their right mind let you go? He asked incredulously.

I responded, "Have you seen Katherine Gold on TV?" By then she had started on "The Rich and The Lost." "She's gorgeous and got voted one of *People Magazine's* 100 Most Beautiful People."

"And?" he said obviously not impressed.

"And she's a knock out!"

"Have you looked in the mirror? Amelia, you are beautiful on so many different levels. I love your beautiful blue eyes, your bright smile, the way you light up a room, but most of all I love who you are. You're honest and I love the fact that you are uncomplicated. There are not many women like you," Shane said emphatically.

I blushed at his complements. What was his angle?" I had wondered.

"I'm going to marry you, Amelia. You're everything I've ever wanted," he said and took my hands in his. "I don't know what this Jett guy's problem was, but I'm glad he let you go. His mistake is my gain," he had professed.

Fifteen years later, I had no regrets and two beautiful children. Shane and I were happy.

"You have a lot more control than I do," Olivia stated. "I'm not sure I would have just walked out without at least telling him he was a dog."

"I haven't spoken to either of them since. I did get an invitation to Jett's wedding and I hear he's happily married," I reported.

"I wouldn't be so generous, I'm afraid," Olivia spoke truthfully.

"I look at the situation as I'm glad I found out before I married him. I would have been devastated if we had been married. It was a blessing!" I said with conviction.

"Did Katherine ever marry?"

I quickly responded, "No and from what the tabloids say, she is dating some 'boy toy' thirteen years her junior. I don't think she will ever settle down. I think her motive was taking Jett away from me. He was a challenge to her, nothing more."

It's funny how time helps us to sort out things and help to make sense of them. That is exactly what Jett had been—a conquest and nothing more. She wanted to prove she could have him.

"Don't worry if she's there. Cassandra and I will handle her," Olivia said with a gleam in her eye.

"Liv, I'm not interested in getting even. It's haunted me long enough. I moved on and I'm happy. I'm the one who won!"

Olivia smiled and continued, "I still don't like her and if I see her I will give her a piece of my mind." Her red head temper was flaring again. "You don't treat your friends like that and get away with it," she said and pounded her fists on the kitchen table for emphasis.

"That's why I have you guys and we are going to have a ball in Dallas. I can't wait to have tea at the Adolphus Hotel!" I shrieked.

"I'm looking forward to that but not as much as going to Fort Worth," Olivia said and pantomimed a country jig.

"Speaking of Dallas and Fort Worth, I better grab Emma and head home to finish packing. Thanks for the tea and can we keep the whole Katherine saga between us?" I requested.

"You can count on me. I can't promise I won't let her have it though if I see her," she laughed.

"Shane doesn't think she will come, so maybe getting worked up is a waste of time," I said rather hopefully.

Olivia and I hugged and headed outside. She had barn chores to finish. I needed to make sure I would look my best at the reunion.

Emma had just finished her lesson and we drove home for a simple salmon dinner with fresh asparagus. For dessert, I had made a strawberry rhubarb pie. It was the last rhubarb of the season and the last meal with my family for a few days.

While Emma and Charlie did their homework, Shane assisted me with getting the suitcases down from the attic. I started laying out my wardrobe for the trip.

"Do you think this dress will be appropriate for the cocktail reception?" I asked holding up a slender black sheath dress. "I thought I would wear my large pearl earrings and sling black pumps," I continued looking at Shane for confirmation of my choice.

"I think you are going to look sensational!" he reassured me. "You aren't trying to dress to impress Jett are you?" he halfway teased.

"I don't even know if he is going and frankly, this isn't about him. I want to make sure I keep up with Cassandra," I smiled.

"You always look good sweetie," he said as he nuzzled the nape of my neck. "Just don't forget who's waiting at home for you."

"How could I ever?" I playfully answered. "When is Aunt Alice getting here?" I asked and started my mental checklist.

"Tomorrow morning around nine so you will have time to go over everything at the tea room with her before you fly out. Don't worry. She's an old pro at this," he said calmly.

And she was. Thank goodness for Shane's Aunt Alice. I could count on her to fill in whenever I had an illness or needed a few days off. She simply followed my carefully detailed recipes and kept the kitchen running in tip top shape. I had also kept reservations to a minimum so she wouldn't be overwhelmed. She had restaurant experience and had run a large commercial kitchen for years. She thought the tea room was "small and cute."

"You make sure Alice has my cell phone number and I will call and check in several times a day to make sure everything goes smoothly," I told him.

"Amelia, this trip is to get your mind off the tea room and to enjoy your friends," he reminded me. "I think Aunt Alice will be just fine. And remember, she can call me and I will be there in five minutes flat. We've got it covered!"

I hoped so as I continued to pack.

FIVE

"Mrs. Reynolds, we'll be landing at Love Field Airport in approximately seven minutes," our pilot announced from the cockpit of the private jet.

"Thank you, Albert!" Cassandra called towards the forward cabin. She was smartly dressed in an aubergine Christian Dior pantsuit. It was something she had picked up in Paris on her last shopping trip. A three stranded black pearl chocker and matching earrings completed the package. She looked as though she had stepped out of the pages of *Vogue*.

"What a wonderful trip and we haven't even landed in Dallas yet," Sarah commented. Traveling in the corporate jet had been a thrill for her. She smiled with contentment as she ran her hands along the buttery leather of her seat.

"How much does a jet like this set you back?" an always practical Olivia asked.

"This is supposed to be a pleasure trip, Liv," Cassandra reminded her. "We are not talking about business this weekend."

"I get it, probably three Riverbend Ranches put together," Olivia continued undaunted. She had dressed for the trip in her black and white snakeskin boots, her Wranglers and a bright yellow Mexican inspired embroidered top. She wore her naturally red hair loose and curly today. A touch of lip gloss and mascara set off her tanned face perfectly.

"We have a car meeting us at the airport. I thought maybe after we check into our rooms, Amelia could give us a tour of Dallas," Cassandra proposed.

"I'm starving!" Olivia broadcasted as she helped herself to another stuffed mushroom cap. "Can we go somewhere Tex Mex?"

"Of course, but I was thinking of an old hangout near campus called Snuffer's," I told her. "They have *the best* cheese fries and burgers anywhere. It's where most of the girls gained the infamous 'freshmen fifteen!'"

"I always worried about the dreaded fifteen pound weight gain when I was at UT," Sarah added as she smoothed her prairie skirt with ruffled petticoat peeking out. Her short sleeved scalloped blouse was adorable.

"It doesn't look like you've ever had to worry about your weight, Sarah," I spoke up. "And remember UT around here will make people think you mean University of Texas."

"Their school colors are also orange and white," Olivia added as she popped another mushroom appetizer in her mouth. "Different shade of orange, more burnt than Tennessee," she mumbled with her mouth full.

"I still can't believe you went to school so far away from home. I don't think I could have done that," Sarah said as she looked out the window down on Dallas laid out like a patchwork quilt below us.

"It's so flat here, no mountain views and very few trees. Perfect for cattle farming and horses," Olivia observed as she joined Sarah by the window.

"Perfect for a cowboy is what you were really thinking!" Cassandra badgered her. "Where there's cattle, there's bound to be a cowboy!"

Albert landed the jet smoothly and within minutes we had taxied to a stop. The flight crew at Love Field airport helped us down the ladder to the waiting town car. Just as soon as our luggage was stowed, we headed downtown to the Adolphus Hotel. I inwardly gasped as we pulled up to the Baroque beauty built in 1912. It had been described as the most beautiful building west of Venice.

"I had no idea when you said we would be staying at a friend's hotel that it would be so grand!" I gushed. And it was from the twenty-one soaring stories to the gorgeous burled wood paneling throughout the lobby. I suddenly felt underdressed wearing a simple black turtleneck cashmere sweater and charcoal gray dress slacks. A tiara and ball gown would have been far more appropriate.

We checked in and were taken up to our luxury suite, our home for the weekend.

"Oh my goodness!" Sarah squealed as we walked through the handsomely appointed living room. "There is a garden terrace! And look, a view of downtown!"

"The round looking orb in the skyline is Reunion Arena," I pointed out to Sarah.

"Have you ever been there? Can you go to the top floor?" she asked almost breathless.

"Yes, you can go to the restaurant on the top floor. The room rotates so the view is constantly changing," I recalled, suddenly feeling wistful. It had been my twenty-first birthday and Jett had surprised me with champagne and a five course meal.

"Sounds romantic, Amelia. What was his name?" Sarah prodded me.

I quickly looked over at Olivia to see if she had let the cat out of the bag about Jett. She raised her eyebrows and shrugged her shoulders indicating she had kept her word.

"No one special," I quickly covered. "It was my twenty-first birthday and a great memory. So who feels like Snuffer's and their world famous cheese fries?" I quickly changed the subject, feeling suddenly stressed.

"Count me in," Olivia raised her hand and brightened considerably.

"Me too," Sarah chimed in.

Snuffer's was a Dallas landmark established in 1978 on Greenville Avenue in close proximity to the SMU campus. The cheddar fries had been called "a rite of passage" by *The Dallas Morning News*. The gigantic hamburgers were legendary. The establishment catered to the lunch crowd mix of college students and local business people. There was nothing quite as exquisite as a hot basket of cheddar cheese fries in my humble opinion.

"Good call, Amelia," Olivia smiled as she licked her fingers. "This is my kind of place." And it was. The laid back atmosphere was a good fit for Olivia's down-to-earth personality. "I haven't seen any cowboys yet," she stated as she took another bite of her burger and looked rather disappointed.

"We will have to go to Fort Worth to meet real cowboys," I laughed.

"On the TV show, *Dallas*, everyone walks around wearing cowboy hats and boots," Sarah pointed out as she took another sip of her sweet iced tea.

"Honey, that was a TV show," Cassandra joked and elbowed Sarah playfully.

"I never saw any cowboys in Dallas though I did see a

lot of boots," I said.

"It's similar to what people think about Tennessee," Cassandra pointed out. "They assume we don't wear shoes and we are all related to Dolly Parton," she jested.

"I can't eat another bite," I groaned and pushed my plate back. "Why don't we walk off our lunch at North Park Mall?" I suggested.

"Is it bigger than the mall at Dogwood Cove?" Sarah asked hopefully as she wiped mustard from the corner of her mouth.

"Oh honey, is it ever!" Cassandra cooed. "They have the very best stores such as Giorgio Armani, Versace and Kate Spade just to name a few. And that's just on the North end of the mall."

"Fine with me as long as you don't try one of your hostile makeovers again," Olivia warned and shot a dirty look out of the corner of her eye in Cassandra's direction.

"I thought you looked stunning after your makeover, Liv," I cajoled her.

"I have been keeping up with the eyebrow waxing," Olivia revealed, "if you haven't noticed."

We sat stunned at her admission. Olivia did care more about her appearance than her hard exterior conveyed. She did have a girly side, but she kept that secret under wraps with most everyone.

"Oh, Liv!" Cassandra squealed as she threw her arms around her. "I am so proud of you!"

"Don't get carried away with the PDA," Olivia cautioned as she untangled herself from Cassandra's embrace. "You're not dressing me in pink like some overenthusiastic Mary Kay sales rep."

"Lighten up and have a little fun, Liv. We could pick out a few new outfits today," Cassandra said optimistically.

Cassandra was undaunted. She strived to push Olivia to reach her true fashion potential. Olivia, on the other hand, was similar in nature to her stubborn mares that dug in their hooves and refused to budge. She didn't see the importance of fashion. In her domain, it was about function.

"If I give in to a new outfit, will you promise not to drag me to Fashion Week with you this year?" Olivia groaned as she rolled her eyes.

"Let's get going before this turns into a bad version of *What Not to Wear*," I suggested as I paid the bill.

Several shopping bags and four hours later, we returned to the hotel exhausted from our excursion.

"If we walked in one more store, I think my feet would have fallen off," Olivia complained as she took off her boots and began rubbing her feet.

"You needed a dress for the cocktail party tomorrow night. How many stores did we peruse until we found 'the one?'" Cassandra reminded her.

"I think six," Sarah estimated. "But we all ended up with great finds. I adore this hand-beaded jewelry. It will compliment many of my outfits. I love it!"

She had made a wise choice. The jewelry suited her carefree spirit and she seemed at the moment much like her old self.

"I'm hanging up my dress for tomorrow night," Olivia beamed as she took her new purchases out of the numerous bags. I noticed she seemed quite proud of herself and couldn't help but exchange a conspirator's grin with Cassandra.

"Before you get busy with your fashion show, I have a little surprise for all of you," Cassandra revealed.

"I hope it doesn't involve walking or I'm going to get blisters for sure," Olivia whined and continued to hang up her dress.

"You don't even have to wear shoes or clothes for that matter," Cassandra said mysteriously as she rubbed her hands together. She was enjoying the suspense.

"No shoes, no clothes? I give up," I admitted defeat and plopped down on the sofa. "I don't care where we go as long as we don't have to move," I groaned.

"Slip into something comfortable and be ready in twenty minutes," she ordered us.

Though we could have easily taken a nap, we were excited about our surprise. After freshening up and changing into more comfortable clothes, we were ready to go. Our car was waiting for us downstairs for the drive to our unknown destination.

"We'll stop here," Cassandra told our driver as he pulled over on McKinney Avenue in the West Village area, a mix of eclectic dining and shops. There was a certain urban vibe to the neighborhood that made it exciting.

"We're taking the McKinney Avenue Trolley to our destination," she revealed.

"How exciting! I've always wanted to ride on an authentic trolley," Sarah exclaimed. It was a great way to see the shops and art galleries.

"Where are we going?" I leaned over and whispered to Cassandra.

"You'll see. Shane and I cooked up this little surprise especially for you," she confessed.

We soon exited at the next trolley stop and found ourselves standing outside of Spa Habitat, voted Dallas' best spa several years in a row. I was speechless. A spa evening! It was definitely what I needed.

I excitedly hugged Cassandra and blurted, "Oh you two thought of everything!" We were ushered through the front door and into a dressing area to change into robes. Our spa hostess, Linda, told us we would be experiencing the "Green Freak" package. It included an organic massage, foot ritual, facial, eco buff and spa dinner. We also would be keeping our robes.

"How did you and Shane pull this off?" I asked amazed. No wonder Shane had been so secretive before I left. I could picture him researching the various spas in Dallas and selecting this one for its environmentally friendly organic products, something we supported in our business as well.

"Shane is the one who read about this spa," Cassandra shared. "He knew how important supporting a green business is to you."

"These robes are organic cotton?" Sarah asked. "They are so comfy. I will enjoy this at home and remember our visit."

"Shane is a keeper, Amelia," Olivia smiled. I knew she was looking for the right person for herself. And she would find him. It would be hard for him to measure up to her high standards and hard work ethic but I knew when Olivia fell, she would fall hard.

"Ladies, which one of you would like to begin your organic body massage now?" Linda asked as she led us down the hallway to the Asian inspired spa treatment rooms. "I can take two of you now for your foot treatments."

A few hours after the foot reflexology, the three stage body buffing with grapefruit mint exfoliating scrub and the hydrating foot and hand treatment, I felt like a limp noodle. I was centered, relaxed and ready for the reunion.

Olivia was impressed. "You have no idea how good it feels to someone who does ranch chores day in and day out!" she purred. "I needed that more than I realized. Why can't we have a spa like this in Dogwood Cove?" she groaned as she stretched her neck.

"Not a bad idea. I would go often," In fact, Shane and I had been working with an aromatherapy specialist to develop a spa line infused with tea. "This would go over well back home."

"I will be having sweet dreams tonight," Sarah yawned and closed her eyes. "I am in a zone of total bliss."

"I am too," Cassandra added. "Linda this has been amazing. Thank you."

The town car was waiting out front and we were all quiet as we drove back to the Adolphus. I was especially reflective this evening wondering who might be attending tomorrow's cocktail party. Little did I know that tonight's serene atmosphere would be the last bit of peace I would experience for quite some time.

SIX

"*I*'ll have a pot of your jasmine pearls," Olivia told the waiter in the grandly appointed French tea salon of the Adolphus Hotel. She looked smart today in one of her new outfits Cassandra had helped her select. The pumpkin colored suede skirt and matching jacket brought out the copper highlights in her hair. She was enjoying herself and the attention she was receiving from the male wait staff.

"Olivia, I am so proud of you," Cassandra boasted and patted her hand affectionately. "No one at home would recognize you out of your Wranglers."

"Let's not get too carried away, Cassandra," Olivia remarked. "I do know how to dress up when the occasion arises as well as dress for work on the ranch."

Olivia was correct about that. I couldn't see her driving her bright green John Deere tractor in those high heeled chocolate brown boots. She did look like a million dollars. I was glad she had given into Cassandra's urging to play dress up while we were shopping yesterday.

"Mmm," I sighed contentedly as I inhaled the malty undertones of the black Assam tea as the waiter filled my cup. I would savor every sip of this heavenly liquid.

Sarah had ordered a pot of spicy Marsala chai while Cassandra was indulging in a Ceylon tea from Sri Lanka flavored with raspberry. Both seemed happy with their selections.

"What a great idea to come here for afternoon tea," Sarah commented as she picked up her pitcher of milk and added a splash to her tea cup. "I just adore chai. The combination of cloves, cardamom, cinnamon and peppercorns remind me of autumn."

"My raspberry tea reminds me of our raspberry filled candies," Cassandra remarked. "This would make a great truffle with the combination of chocolate and raspberry."

"I agreed wholeheartedly. Tea infused truffles were quite a trend in both the chocolate and tea worlds. In fact, tea-infused foods were served in several of the trend setting restaurants in Hollywood, Boston, New York and DC.

"Amelia, between your knowledge of tea and my knowledge of chocolate, it would seem only natural to collaborate on a line of tea-infused candies," Cassandra proposed.

"I would be the first in line to try them," Sarah said delighted at the idea. She looked quite chick today in a red suit with faux fur collar and cuffs, a tribute to 'Jackie-O'. She completed the look with a black jet bead broach, black gloves and vintage patent leather handbag. She was a throwback to the 1960's and wore it well. All she needed was a pillbox hat.

"Shane and I have been looking into developing other products featuring our teas," I shared. "I think adding tea infused chocolates is a grand idea. I have tried several different varities on our afternoon tea trays and they have been overwhelmingly popular with our guests." I took another sip of Assam and felt my shoulders relax as I enjoyed the company surrounding me.

"Are you talking about those chocolates you gave me for

my birthday last year?" Olivia recalled as her eyes lit up.

"Those were the orange blossom oolong truffles," I answered. I loved the way the tea was blended with orange blossoms not only scenting the tea but adding to its exotic flavor. It paired well with dark chocolate and made a very distinct and memorable flavor combination.

"Those were so wonderful, I didn't even want to share them," Olivia divulged and looked sheepishly around the table. She had eaten the entire box in a matter of hours.

"We noticed, Liv," Cassandra jested. "We were all hoping to try one, but I guess we'll just wait until our next birthday."

I loved the way this tight knit group could banter back and forth, but still have so much love between the four of us.

"To 'The Traveling Tea Ladies,'" I toasted and we each raised our tea cups and gently clanked them together.

Our waiter presented our table with a gorgeous three-tiered tea tray layered with currant scones served with Devonshire cream and lemon curd. There were thinly sliced cucumber tea sandwiches, smoked salmon with capers and a lovely selection of pastries and tarts. The blueberry sour cream tart was by far my favorite.

"Oh my stars," Cassandra gushed. "This has been so wonderful and I am captivated by the ambiance of this dining room. I wish I could find out who their decorator is and hire them!"

"Your house looks like a miniature version of Versailles as it is, Cassandra," I reminded her. "You don't need any help decorating or re-decorating."

We all nodded our heads in agreement. Cassandra had any eye for color, furniture placement and table scapes. Many Reynolds's contract negotiations had been held in the living room of her Dogwood Cove home. It wasn't un-usual to find Cassandra and Doug entertaining one of their celebrity friends on the weekends in their majestic lakefront mansion.

"Speaking of Versailles, I am planning a trip in the spring to Paris to develop new recipes for Reynolds's."

"Oooh la la and kiss my grits," Olivia teased.

"Maybe you should think about coming with me and developing your tea truffles with our head chef," she propo-sitioned. It was obvious she was serious about her offer.

"Do you mean it?" I couldn't believe the opportunity she was extending. I didn't know what to think.

"Of course I mean it. This isn't the first time I've thought about it and with your tea education and culinary experience, this would be a sure fire best seller," Cassandra predicted.

For the first time in the last few weeks I felt excited. I had been focusing solely on what I was saying goodbye to and had not realized how much I had to look forward to.

"Girls, this calls for champagne," Olivia declared. "We have a lot to toast."

"I'll say," Sarah agreed. "How exciting Amelia. If you hadn't decided to sell the Pink Dogwood Tea Room, this opportunity may not have presented itself."

Sarah was right. I was beginning to see a bright future in which I would be working with Shane on a daily basis and stretching my creativity. And a definite perk was working surrounded by the delightful aroma of tea and now chocolate. I was beginning to brighten at the prospect.

I felt a lift in my step as we returned to our suite to get ready for the cocktail party to be held at the Meadows Museum on the SMU campus. The museum held a special place in my heart as I had spent my undergraduate days working there as an intern in marketing. I fell in love with the Spanish Golden Age collection that included works by Goya, Murillo and Picasso.

My job had been to write press releases for upcoming art shows and to help catalogue the artwork for the museum. There was a beautiful sculpture garden in the plaza featuring bronzes by Rodin. It would be the perfect backdrop for a cocktail party.

Our hotel suite was large enough to accommodate the primping needs of four ladies. We all took turns zipping dresses, fastening necklaces and assisting each other with makeup. Olivia had even consented to eyeliner tonight.

I found myself especially nervous, not quite sure who would be there. But I was confident with my good friends by my side, the evening would be fine. I hoped it would be.

My black sleeveless sheath dress was elegantly understated. I wore my hair in a simple upsweep reminiscent of Grace Kelly. I looked with approval in the mirror as I carefully put on my pearl and diamond earrings. A matching black wrap completed the outfit. I was ready for whatever the evening held.

"Are we ready ladies?" Cassandra asked the group. She looked stunning in a champagne colored pantsuit with a textured tapestry jacket and silk top. The honey highlights in her hair stood out even more than usual. An antique pearl broach and cascading strands of pearls and Swarovski crystals finished the ensemble. She oozed class.

"I'm ready," Olivia answered. She was wearing an emerald green velvet cocktail dress with her down in loose spiral curls. She reminded me of a petite version of Nicole Kidman tonight with her clear complexion, fiery red hair and tiny frame.

Sarah joined us wearing a highly embellished Indian sari in variations of gold and burgundy. Her black silk dress pants and gold gladiator sandals kept the look updated and dressy for tonight's affair.

"Sarah, I never would have thought of wearing that. You look fantastic!" I blurted out as she entered the room.

"It's comfortable and exotic at the same time," she smiled and enjoyed the flattery.

"You're not going to break out in the dance of seven veils, are you?" Olivia joked and began spinning around the room holding a hotel towel as if it were a veil in front of her face.

"I've been taking belly dancing classes on Tuesday night and I'm becoming quite good," Sarah boasted as she swung her hips from side to side.

"Sarah, I've never seen this side of you," I said surprised. We all started dancing around the room attempting to follow Sarah's instructions.

"If only Shane and Doug could see us now. They would be rolling in the floor. We better high tail it before our coach turns into a pumpkin," Cassandra reminded us as we tried our best to catch our breath. Who knew belly dancing could be such great exercise?

The drive from downtown to the SMU campus was a relatively short one. As dusk approached, the entrance to the school at Mockingbird Lane and Bishop Boulevard was lit as if a Hollywood director had waited for just the right moment to create the perfect shot. Ancient oak trees lined the lane leading your eye to the centerpiece, Dallas Hall. Built in 1911 and fashioned after Thomas Jefferson's Rotunda on the

University of Virginia campus, it was a spectacular sight to behold. Its rounded copper roof had aged to a mellow patina.

"How beautiful," Sarah said softly as she gazed out the window of the car. "I can't believe you went to school here."

Our driver circled the complete horseshoe of Bishop Boulevard to let us take in the view of this unique property. He stopped in front of Dallas Hall, majestically lit. The massive fountain bubbled in front of the expansive lawn. I felt an involuntary lump in my throat as I recalled the classes I had taken in those hallowed halls and how I had enjoyed feeling as though I was walking in the footsteps of history.

We slowly continued driving past Perkins Chapel where so many weddings had taken place on campus. Many couples who wed there had met as undergraduates at SMU. There were many Saturday afternoons when I had witnessed happy wedding parties exiting the chapel in a hail of rice. It was where Jett and I had planned on having our own wedding ceremony.

Valet attendants were waiting to open the doors to our town car as we approached Meadows Museum. We were ushered upstairs to the party already in progress.

Olivia gently took my elbow and whispered in my ear, "Remember Amelia, I have your back," she winked as a sign of her support.

"Thanks Liv," and I truly meant it. My stomach was doing flip flops at this point. I concentrated on making it up the steps without too many bumbles.

"Ladies may I take a picture for the alumni newsletter?" a young man with a tripod requested at the museum entrance.

We stood together with our arms around each other. "Remember girls. It's one, two, and three, tea!" I instructed them.

"Tea," we called out in chorus.

As we stepped inside the entrance, we were greeted by a registration table with name tags laid out.

"Welcome Class of 1990!" a platinum blonde Miss Texas look-a-like enthusiastically greeted us. "If y'all will tell me your names, I'll find your badges."

"I hate these things," Olivia complained as she pinned her nametag on her top. "Maybe I don't want everyone knowing my name. You can't be too careful these days." She was still frowning as she smoothed her dress.

"Liv, I don't think anyone here will bother you. This isn't a honky-tonk bar. It's a nice function," Cassandra chided her. "The men here might be a tad more respectable."

"You can never be certain," Olivia mumbled and shot me a conspirator's glance.

"I can just imagine you as a student walking around this museum surrounded by all this fine art," Sarah said in awe.

"Back then, this museum had not been built. Everything was housed in the Owens Art Center. This museum is a new addition to the school," I shared with her.

I had brought Shane here during my last visit. We both had enjoyed perusing the different galleries showcasing the largest collection of Spanish art outside of Spain from the 1550's to Picasso. Right now I wished he were here by my side. By now, I was missing my family. I was having a wonderful time, but it would have been even more perfect with all of them here.

Our foursome walked into the main foyer. There were several bars set up including one area dedicated solely to tequila tasting, similar to a wine tasting. There were subtle variations in each of the tequilas depending on the maker, the maker's process and the Blue Agave's growing environment. Tonight the bartender was serving eight featured tequilas in a tulip shaped wine glass with plenty of tortillas and water for cleansing the palate between sampling.

"No thank you," Olivia politely told the server who offered her a glass of Pepe Lopez. "The last time I had tequila I rode the mechanical bull at The Lazy Spur and nearly broke my back," she reminded me. She scared all of us that night. It had turned out to be a mild case of whiplash and soon she was back in the saddle again. Yes, maybe it was wise to avoid the tequila.

As we strolled along the gallery, there was a maze of different rooms featuring various artists and their collections. In the center of each room were tables draped in black linens with a tempting array of hors d'oeuvres. I helped myself to a wonderful blue cheese and apricot spread on rye cocktail bread and continued to explore the exhibit.

"Amelia, you need to try the stuffed figs. They are scrumptious!" Sarah said enthusiastically as she took a bite. She looked stunning in her sari. I admired her willingness to take risks with her wardrobe and her zest for life. There was nothing phony about her child-like innocence. She appeared to be enjoying the trip and was in much better spirits. I hoped she had decided what to do about her library position.

"Is this a Picasso?" she asked with her eyes widening in disbelief. "I have never seen one in person."

I turned to admire the abstract alongside Sarah when I sensed someone behind us. I assumed it was Cassandra and Olivia as I turned quickly, smiling to include them.

"Amelia, I thought that was you. You look beautiful." Standing before me was Jett Rollins, all six foot three inches of him. I momentarily stood there dumbfounded. I had hoped he wouldn't attend and wasn't prepared myself to see him again.

I had to admit, he looked good. He was a bit gray around the temples of his dark brown hair and not quite as thin as he had been in college. His lavender dress shirt brought out the blue in his eyes and contrasted nicely with his black suit. He appeared fit as if he had kept up his workout routine from years of running track.

"Hello, I'm Sarah," she said quickly extending her hand and giving Jet a warm smile. "I'm Amelia's friend from Dogwood Cove." Thank goodness for Sarah's unswerving manners. This allowed time for me to compose myself.

"Nice to see you Jett," I spoke in a controlled monotone not conveying a hint of surprise or emotion. "Where is Laura?"

"She's at home with the twins," he informed us and took out his cell phone to show pictures. "They were born nine weeks ago."

He proudly showed pictures of his stunning wife, a former Miss Kentucky, holding two babies in her arms. One baby was swaddled in pink, the other in blue. "Jacob and Bonnie," he said softly. "We weren't sure we could have children. But here are our precious miracles."

"Congratulations Jett. What a beautiful family you have," I said with all sincerity.

"What about your family? I read in the alumni news about the birth of your children. How old are they now?"

"Emma is fourteen and Charlie is twelve. Shane is home with the kids and handling some business while I'm here with my good friends," I politely answered.

Cassandra and Olivia walked up to join our intimate circle. Olivia glanced at Jett's name badge and recognition set in. She raised her eyebrows in confirmation as she looked directly at me.

"Jett Rollins, these are my good friends, Olivia Rivers and Cassandra Reynolds."

"Hello Jett," Cassandra said nonchalantly. "I'm pleased to meet you." It was obvious to me that she had no idea about the history between us. She had heard Shane mention his name in reference as an old boyfriend, but nothing more.

"Jett," Olivia said coldly and gave him a curt nod. She turned away as if she were far more interested in the painting behind her. I was amused by Olivia's behavior. She couldn't pretend to tolerate someone she didn't respect.

"Amelia and I were catching up on our families," he told them.

"Yes, Amelia has a *wonderful* husband who *adores* her and two precious children. She is very *lucky* and extremely *happy*," Olivia bellowed. Jett looked slightly taken aback by her forcefulness.

"That's all I ever wanted for her," he declared as he glanced in my direction. Remorse was written all over his face. It was apparent to me he was feeling bad for the way things had ended between us.

"Jett was showing us pictures of his wife Laura and their beautiful newborn twins," I said casting a conspicuous look in Olivia's direction. There was no need for her to be so combative. I doubted she would stop.

"Congratulations!" Cassandra smiled. "Is Laura here with you tonight?" she said looking expectantly around to meet his wife.

"No, she's at home with the babies but insisted I come," he said politely. "I was hoping to see you and maybe if you have time later, we could continue to catch up," he whispered turning his full attention to me.

"Yoo hoo, Amelia!" I heard from across the gallery. "I knew you would be here!"

"Leslie Lane!" I squealed and gave her an enthusiastic hug. Leslie had majored in theater. She and Katherine had always competed for the lead in the department's productions. The three of us had shared a rental house our junior and senior years. Leslie and I had kept close and she had been my maid of honor at my wedding.

"Jett Rollins ... well, well, well." Leslie's voice dripped with sarcasm. "Long time no see. I guess the last time I saw you, Jett, you were caught with your pants down!"

"Leslie, I see you haven't lost your charm," Jett fired back. This little exchange between the two was making everyone uncomfortable. "Ladies if you'll excuse me. Amelia, I hope we have the chance to catch up later," he reminded me as he quickly walked away.

"Leslie, I can't believe you are here. You look gorgeous!" I exclaimed as I took in her smoldering cat-like green eyes and black hair. She had been the envy of many coeds at SMU. The years had done little to change her. Tonight she was wearing a black strapless dress, her ample bosom barely contained. She wore a Cleopatra inspired gold asp bracelet, its green eyes mirroring her own.

I often wondered why she had not made it big in the movie world. She had talent, was a gifted singer, dancer and actress and a Tony Award winner. She was waiting for her big break. Shane and I recently had seen her perform in

Wicked. She was extraordinary!

"I flew in from New York this afternoon. I couldn't miss the opportunity to see everyone again," she said and squeezed my hands. Leslie had been the one to pack all my belongings and put them in storage so I wouldn't have to come back to the house and confront Katherine. She had been a loyal friend.

"Leslie, you remember Olivia, Sarah and Cassandra?"

"Hi, girls! How have you been?" she said kissing each of them warmly on the cheek. "Cassandra I haven't seen you since the Tony Awards."

"Wasn't that fun? I think Hugh Jackman did a wonderful job hosting this year."

"Oh, I forgot the two of you travel in the same circles," Olivia said mockingly and rolled her eyes. "Hugh Jackman, George Clooney, Angelina Jolie ..."

"Katherine Gold," Leslie interrupted as the paparazzi cameras began flashing, snapping pictures of Katherine's grand entrance into the museum.

She wore a white fur stole draped around the shoulders of her body-hugging gold Versace gown. It was cut dangerously low in the back and high at the thigh. It was obvious double sided tape had been carefully placed in strategic areas. She looked smoking hot tonight and her body language indicated she knew she owned the room.

"Katherine, Katherine, over here!" the paparazzi called out to her. "Show us your dress. Who are you wearing tonight?"

"She's wearing Versace," a stern woman dressed in a navy pinstriped business suit addressed the TV crews. Her conservative low heeled pumps and bobbed hair were a sharp contrast to Katherine's six inch gold stilettos and long gold mane. "If you'll hurry and take a few more shots of Miss Gold so she can enjoy her reunion please," the woman barked.

Katherine was eating up the attention. She posed with her back towards the cameras and gave a vampy look over her shoulder. She turned her leg out to the side to expose her famous gams while blowing kisses at her admirers.

"Thank you, thank you. If you'll let Miss Gold through now," the efficient woman shouted as she led Katherine through the doorway.

"Is that her?" Olivia asked me. "I think her dress screams desperate. If she doesn't watch it, she may have a wardrobe malfunction," she joked referring to Janet Jackson's Super Bowl snafu a few years ago.

"I concur one hundred percent, Olivia," Leslie said snidely. "Look at her, so needy for attention."

Leslie had a point. After living with Katherine for a few years, I knew her quite well. Anytime we had company over, male or female, Katherine insisted on being the center of attention—especially male attention. There had been more than one of Leslie's dates who had fallen victim to her wily ways. Over the years, she had learned not to bring her anyone home or arrange to have them over when Katherine was away.

"She's like a praying mantis," Leslie elaborated. "She devours every male in her path."

"Enough about her," I interrupted as I realized my stomach was tied in knots. "I think I will try that tequila bar," I said heading in the opposite direction of the throng of Katherine Gold fan club members who followed her around like a litter of puppies.

"Wait up, I'm coming too," Olivia cried after me. I was

glad she was there for the support. Sarah and Cassandra continued their conversation with Leslie and waved goodbye at us from across the gallery.

"Two Pepe Lopez's please," I requested from the bartender.

"I like Leslie. She's a straight shooter," Olivia commented.

"Much like you," I agreed as we clinked glasses. "I wish I could disappear," I revealed.

"Don't be ridiculous," Olivia reproved me. "If anyone should be embarrassed to be at this reunion, it should be Katherine. You didn't get caught with your roommate's fiancée. You didn't plunge a dagger into your friends back. You didn't break up an engagement. She did and she should be ashamed to show her face after what she did to you!" Olivia ranted, her fiery temper stoked. Tequila may not have been a good idea after all.

"Thank you, sweetie," I said warmly and kissed her cheek. "You've always known the right thing to say."

"It's obvious Jett feels bad. But that doesn't excuse his behavior. You know how I feel about cheating, but from what the tabloids print, no man can say no to Katherine Gold," Olivia fumed. "She's been linked to everyone from Tom Cruise to Brad Pitt. She's a home wrecker," she declared as she finished her tequila and slammed her glass down. She headed towards the shrimp wrapped bacon appetizer and popped one into her mouth as she stacked three more on a small white plate.

"Have you ever thought Jett has regrets?" She implied as she looked compassionately at me.

"I think he has regrets, like he regrets being caught." I often wondered if he would have told me had I not walked in on them. "Quite frankly, it doesn't matter. I don't regret what happened. It was a blessing. Shane and the kids are my whole life," I divulged.

"You were lucky Amelia. You ended up with happily-ever-after. I'm not so sure Katherine has found hers yet," she said with authority in her voice. "That young Hollywood 'boy-toy' she's dating is using her to further his career. You can bet on that!"

"When did you become such an expert on celebrity gossip?" I teased.

"I read *People* and *US Weekly*," she admitted sheepishly. "Just don't let Cassandra know. She'd never let me live it down since I give her such a hard time about her 'Holly-weird' friends,'" she chuckled and quickly consumed another shrimp. "I'm starving. Don't they have a prime rib or something substantial around here?" she whined.

"Olivia and her hearty appetite!" Cassandra announced siding up to us. She fluffed Olivia's spiral curls and continued. "Sarah and I were just having a nice chat with Leslie. She's going to audition for a new movie next week. I think she's nervous about this one. Ron Howard is directing it," Cassandra informed me.

"Ron Howard? I would be nervous too," I agreed.

"I am hoping to get Leslie to Dogwood Cove to do an evening with the symphony orchestra. It would be a sold-out show for certain," Cassandra predicted.

"That's a great idea. I would love for her to come to Dogwood Cove again. It's been a few years since she last visited. I think an invitation from Cassandra Reynolds would carry some clout," I giggled.

"I'll keep working on her. Are you OK Amelia?" she

turned facing me. "Leslie filled me in on Jett and Katherine. It sounds like it was a horrible time for you. Why didn't you tell me when I was out at your place the other night? I could just shoot myself for going on and on about you and Katherine being roommates," she lamented.

"It's ancient history. I don't want you to feel bad about bringing her up. It's a topic I would rather not discuss but that mess was over twenty years ago. Shane and I are such a perfect fit. I feel as though everything has happened for a reason," I reassured her.

"She's a better woman than I," Olivia interrupted. "I personally would have tossed Katherine Gold out by her Goldilocks!" Olivia erupted loudly. The catering attendant looked over at us.

"Olivia, keep it down," I warned through gritted teeth. "People are looking at you."

"No more tequila for her," Cassandra smiled and told the caterer. She led Olivia away from the table. "Let's find you some coffee," she suggested.

"I have had two tequilas. I'm fine, mother!" Olivia bristled at the suggestion. "I am hungry though."

"I saw a coffee bar over in the far gallery," Sarah told us.

"Lead the way," I said as we followed her into one of the smaller back gallery rooms.

"A-ME-LI-A! Amelia Spencer!" a high pitched voice called out.

I turned and saw Holly Smith running across the room. She tripped slightly but steadied herself and made her way to embrace me.

"Holly, what a surprise!"

"You knew I wouldn't miss the reunion. Will you be here

for the big homecoming game against Rice tomorrow?" she inquired hopefully.

"Yes we will. Holly, let me introduce you to my good friends from Dogwood Cove. Cassandra Reynolds, Olivia Rivers and Sarah McCaffrey," I acquainted them. "Holly was our Gamma Phi Beta President and a real 'go-getter,' " I informed them. She was border-line pesky at times, but she had shaped our sorority into one of the largest chapters in the southwest.

"Nice to meet all of you," she said with an exuberant smile pasted on her face. She looked as though she were still actively recruiting for rush week. "I must insist all of you stop by the house tomorrow morning for a pre-game sorority brunch. The girls would love to have you and all of our alumnae will be in attendance," she said rather insistently.

Great. Katherine had been in my pledge class. I hoped she would be sleeping in or too busy to come.

"Of course Katherine Gold will be there! We can't have our most famous sister in town and not have her drop by the house. The girls are thrilled to meet her!" she bounced up and down like an aged cheerleader. Typical Holly—full of spirit!

"I'll try to make it," I smiled and attempted to change the subject. "Have you seen Leslie Lane tonight? She's here and it sounds as if she's going to be filming a movie soon."

"Really? I simply must find her and invite her to the brunch. Tootles!" she called out to us.

"Tootles! Ta, tah!" Olivia replied. "Is she oblivious to everything and everyone?" she observed.

"No she's a former sorority girl who thinks she's still in the middle of rush," I replied and chortled.

"You wouldn't catch me joining a sorority," Olivia opined. "I wouldn't pay to belong to a clique."

"You do have a way with words, Olivia. I'll have you know I was a Tri-Delta!" Cassandra informed her outspoken friend.

"I should have guessed. That explains a lot," she snorted and poked Cassandra in the ribs.

"Are you going to go tomorrow? I wouldn't let Katherine keep me from enjoying old friends," Sarah advised.

"Truer words have never been spoken," Cassandra agreed.

We stood around the coffee bar as we sipped cappuccinos. Olivia helped herself to the chocolate covered espresso beans.

"Watch it," Cassandra warned her. "You'll be up all night."

"Thanks for the warning, Mom!" Olivia snarked.

As we turned around to find a table, we ran smack dab into the 'praying mantis' herself and her embattled assistant.

"If it isn't little Miss Amelia Spencer from Poe-dunk Cove Tennessee," Katherine sneered as she looked me over from head-to-toe. "I can't believe you found something to wear for the cocktail party. Oh, I forgot, you have a Wal-Mart in 'Hicksville' with a formalwear selection next to the auto parts," she triumphed.

"Her husband was right when he said you were a real witch," Cassandra responded standing toe-to-toe with Katherine. "I've heard stories about you in Hollywood and if half of what they say about you is true, your career is a total wash up. It's a shame your contract with *The Rich and the Lost* is not being renewed," Cassandra scoffed.

Katherine looked shocked as her mouth hung open. Cassandra had hit a nerve but that didn't deter her.

"Speaking of your husband, where is he?" she panto-mimed looking around the room for someone. "Let me guess, you couldn't hold on to him too," she taunted.

"Ladies, ladies, let's keep this down," the pinstriped suit pleaded. "We don't want this conversation becoming tomor-row's headlines," her assistant emphasized.

"Then tell 'Miss Femme Fatale' to apologize to my friend," Cassandra recommended. I had never seen her so angry before.

"Apologize for what?" Katherine spat. "Apologize for saving her from that boring boyfriend of hers? She's better off. He was like clay in my capable hands," she bragged and looked in my direction was a smug grin on her face.

"Katherine, that's enough! Get a grip on yourself and have some decency about yourself," Jett roared.

With all the chaos going on, I had not seen Jett ap-proach the coffee bar. By now, all the caterers and servers were standing around gawking. This had turned into an ugly scene with no escape in sight.

"Oh classic! 'Dudley-Do-Right' arrives to save the dam-sel in distress. She's always had her friends rescuing her," she complained.

It was then I realized Olivia was correct. Katherine wasn't really happy. She had fame, a beautiful body and money, but she wasn't truly happy. You can have it all and still feel all alone. And from the way she was behaving, I couldn't see her maintaining a relationship with anyone for long. Maybe that was why she attempted to take other people's happiness. She was a miserable human being.

"Katherine, let's go. You've said enough for one night," the suit chided her. As her assistant rushed her out the door, the photographers followed snapping pictures of her hasty retreat. We were all shell shocked wondering what had just taken place.

Leslie approached me and clasped her arms around me. "Don't fret. That's as bad as she gets. All bark and no bite, remember?" she joked.

"Cassandra is it true what you said about her contract?" I asked. If it were true, Katherine had to be devastated. She had landed the job straight out of college. Primarily it was what she had been doing the last twenty years.

"It's true," she replied. "Ratings are down and budgets are being slashed. She's a highly paid soap star." I had forgotten Cassandra was a friend with the Bowman's who created, directed and produced the soap.

"And now she's a former soap queen who has been typecast," Leslie predicted.

"If her assistant was worried about tomorrow's headlines, maybe she put a lock on her mouth," Olivia pointed out the obvious.

"Her assistant is her sister, Monica," Leslie told us.

"That was Monica Gold?" I asked in disbelief. "The last time I saw her she was getting ready to graduate from high school. She used to come and visit on the weekends," I explained to the girls.

"I don't envy her working with Katherine," Sarah empathized "For me that would be a miserable existence."

"I don't know about the rest of you, but I could go for a steak. Is there a good steakhouse nearby?" Olivia asked addressing the group. "Let's blow this popsicle stand!"

"I've got an idea. Leslie, join us!" I insisted as I excused myself and made a quick call to Dakota's, a chic downtown

Dallas spot located eighteen feet underground.

The ride down on the elevator was worth a trip there just to see the waterfalls. The restaurant had an interesting history. Since it was built on the First Baptist Dallas Church property, it had a legally binding clause that no alcohol could be served on the premises. In order to serve wine and spirits, the owners decided to go one block below street level to build the establishment. I was pleased they had a table for five available and would hold it for us.

"Good night Jett," I told him. "Thanks for interceding on my behalf, but I don't need you to do that. You don't owe me a thing."

"I'm sorry, Amelia. I'm sorry for everything. If I could go back in time, I would change it all," he said sincerely. He looked downtrodden.

"You wouldn't have Laura and those beautiful babies and I wouldn't have my family. It was meant to be, no regrets. I want you to know how happy I am and happy with my life. I can't imagine living any other way," I reassured him.

"I'm glad to hear it and to know you have good friends," he said smiling around at the girls surrounding us. "I feel better knowing everything turned out well for you."

"Be happy," I told him and turned and walked out of the museum.

SEVEN

"Have you seen the headlines this morning?" Sarah asked as she shook me awake. "You need to read this."

"Hmm. What time is it? My alarm clock hasn't gone off yet," I mumbled and yawned as I sat up in bed. "What's so important that it can't wait for coffee or at least a strong pot of Irish breakfast tea?"

"It's Katherine Gold. She is the headline in the *Dallas Morning News* today," she quietly informed me.

"What now? Wasn't her performance last night enough?" I asked grabbing the paper. The front page featured a picture of Katherine at last night's gala posing seductively. The headline read "SMU Grad is Good as Gold." How annoying.

"She's lucky no reporters overheard the argument last night with Cassandra. If the details of her defunct contract leaked out, there would be a much different headline," I said tossing the paper to the side and getting slowly out of bed. What a way to start the morning.

"I'm sure her sister made certain there was no negative press," Sarah opined. "She will make sure she spins everything in the best light."

"I'll read it later. Coffee first," I said over my shoulder as I headed towards the bathroom.

"Don't bother reading it," Olivia said haughtily as she plopped herself down on the bed still wearing her pajamas. "It's a bunch of horse hockey about how successful Katherine is, how she is the highest paid soap opera actress and more nonsense about her latest love affair with 'boy toy' Conrad Ryan. I think I'm going to toss my cookies," Olivia moaned as she rolled on the bed. "Amelia, she's going to receive the Distinguished Alumni Award at today's game. Who'd she have to sleep with to get that distinction, I wonder?" Olivia snickered.

I stuck my head outside the bathroom door and laughed at Olivia's commentary. "From what Cassandra says, this may be her last hoorah. Let her have it. I'm taking a nice hot shower!"

Shortly thereafter I joined the girls in the living room. Olivia was sitting on the couch wearing her traditional Wranglers, red ostrich boots, embroidered blue shirt and a matching red cowgirl hat. Her large silver belt buckle was studded with turquoise. It was her Santa Fe rendition of wearing SMU school colors. She looked darling.

Cassandra hung up the phone and joined us. "That was my friend, Melissa Bowman, the producer of *The Rich and the Lost*," she revealed and looked like a cat caught swallowing the canary.

"What, what did she say? Tell us!" Sarah pleaded as she joined Olivia on the sofa. She was dressed as if she were attending a 50's sock hop wearing a red and blue varsity-style sweater, rolled up blue jeans and a pair of saddle oxfords for today's game against Rice.

"Melissa confirmed Katherine has been let go from the show. Her last episode airs in two weeks. Rumor has it she is considering relocating to Dallas. She's been sending out demos to the local stations to pitch a show similar to *Entertainment Tonight* called *The Talk of Texas*," Cassandra divulged.

"No wonder Monica is being so careful about the press. Today's headline will get her into the right country clubs, social contacts and job opportunities for sure," Olivia inferred.

"You need to read the article Amelia," Sarah insisted handing me the paper. "She has managed to make herself out to be a cross between Mother Teresa and Reese Witherspoon. She has done a great job of creating a phony history."

"Don't worry, it will catch up with her eventually," Cassandra reasoned. "You know what they say about Karma baby!" She was dressed in a chic suede skirt with matching tan boots and a long sleeved cobalt shirt. Cassandra was not the type to wear jeans unless she was camping, so her ensemble today was no surprise to me.

"I'm looking forward to showing you ladies around campus and attending the game. I think Katherine will be so busy with her spin doctors and paparazzi we will probably not even cross paths with her," I hoped aloud.

After last night I was quickly reminded how ugly she could be. Her insulting comments and her need to inflict pain took me back twenty years to our days together on campus. It wasn't enough that every guy practically stumbled over their own feet to turn and watch her walk by. She craved every man's attention. There had been more arguments at the Gamma Phi Beta house about Katherine's behavior at our social events. I wasn't the only one who had lost her beau to Katherine over the years.

I had been a good friend and roommate to her. I constantly defended that friendship to our sorority sisters who were upset with the attention she was dominating. "You know Katherine is a flirt. She doesn't even realize what she is doing. She would never hurt a friend," I had reasoned with the girls on several occasions. I could kick myself now for being such a fool! I thought had been protecting her and actually, I had enabled her poor behavior. I was part of the problem. Now her sister Monica was taking up where I had left off.

Talking with Jett last night had brought closure regarding what had happened. His apology, though a tad bit overdue, needed to be said. Knowing he had regrets about his involvement with Katherine helped me to move on. I would never again look back at my years at SMU with a knot in my stomach. I was no longer a victim. I felt suddenly empowered. That naïve girl from Dogwood Cove had been replaced with a confident woman.

Our chauffeur was waiting at the entrance to the hotel. A short drive later, we were standing in front of the massive white columns of the Gamma Phi Beta house on sorority row. Homecoming banners and welcome signs were draped across the facade.

"This looks more like a mansion than a sorority house," Olivia remarked as we walked into the entry. We were greeted by the current residents who courteously ushered us into the dining room. A long buffet had been set up with steam tables filled with various breakfast offerings.

"They have ranchos huevos!" Olivia cried. The combination of corn tortillas, eggs, salsa, refried beans and jalapenos was a Texas staple. "It's hard to find good ranchos huevos in Dogwood Cove. I'm as happy as a clam."

"Ladies, help yourselves," Holly greeted us. She had on the Gamma Phi Beta colors of pink and brown and her recruiting attitude was on full display. "It's so good to see y'all this morning. Amelia, did you see *The Dallas Morning News* today? Your former roommate is once again in the headlines. We're hoping reporters will show up for her visit to Gamma Phi this morning as well," Holly gushed and smiled her trademark animated grin.

"Great, a visit from 'Cruella DeVille,'" Olivia muttered under her breath. She quickly loaded her plate with hash browns and a large cinnamon roll. We made our way over to the decorated tables in the adjoining room.

"Good morning everyone!" Leslie called out and waved at our group. "May I join you for breakfast?"

"Absolutely," Cassandra answered as she motioned to an empty chair next to her.

"Miss Lane, I'm a huge fan. Can I have your autograph?" a young doe eyed coed asked politely.

"Of course," she beamed and signed several autographs while she was at the house that morning. Leslie was very humble and always took time for her fans. I admired that about her.

Holly went around the dining room handing out pledge promises to each of the alumnae. "Mrs. Reynolds, we would be pleased if you considered a one-time gift to the Gamma Phi Beta foundation. It inspires leadership skills in young women and also goes towards our charity summer camps for underprivileged children," she recited loudly.

"Thank you Holly, I will look over this and mail it back to you," Cassandra politely replied.

"She was a Tri Delta Delta something," Olivia spoke up.

"I don't quite understand the Greek system, but it means she was in a rival sorority," Olivia explained and struggled to keep a straight face as she continued eating.

"We encourage sisterhood between all sororities on campus. There's no rivalry going on between the Tri Deltas and Gamma Phi on our part," Holly responded in a slightly irritated tone. "Amelia, have you made out your will and bequeathed your gift to Gamma Phi?"

I swallowed hard and looked up at her hovering over me. "I will discuss that with Shane after the reunion, in private," I cautioned her. She was being overbearing this morning. I realized it was important for us to remain donors, but this was a matter not to be discussed in front of my friends. She had put me on the spot and I didn't appreciate her overzealousness.

"I'll call you after the reunion for a follow up," she chirped and moved on to the next table of alumnae.

"She reminds me of the Grim Reaper," Olivia said in shock. "It's not enough to come right out and ask Cassandra for money, but to point blank ask you about your will is a little weird to me," she spewed and pushed back her plate. "I'm ready to go," she abruptly announced.

I had to agree with Olivia. I too was ready to go. Holly had always been pushy. I suddenly wondered about her personal life. I had not thought to ask her at the cocktail party. We had only talked about the sorority and Katherine.

"Let's hurry up before we have a repeat of last night," I instructed the girls. We were all in agreement. It was time to go. We stood up and began walking towards the door.

"Before you go, let me give you passes for the VIP skybox," Holly said handing each of us a blue pass with a red mustang on the front. "We can't have someone as important as Cassandra Reynolds sitting in general seating, can we?"

Olivia rolled her eyes and Cassandra pinched her elbow to try and get her to not be quite so obvious. "Thank you, that's very generous," she responded politely.

"Leslie, come with us to the parade," I encouraged her.

"I would love to, but I'm singing the National Anthem at kickoff. I have to get to the stadium early to warm up but I can meet you in the skybox later."

"It's a plan. Break a leg," I told her and gave her a squeeze. We were finally off to the parade and it was good timing since the sidewalks along Hill Crest Avenue were already filled with underclassmen dressed in red and blue. Police escorts signaled the parade's start followed by Peruna, the official mascot, shaking hands with the children along the parade route.

The school mascot was decided when a past president's assistant commented that the football team looked like a 'bunch of wild mustangs' out on the field. The student body adopted the symbol and gave the mustang the nickname Peruna after a patented tonic with a high alcoholic kick to it. There had been an instantiated rumor that Ford Motor Company had named their car model after the mighty SMU football team.

"Look girls," Olivia squealed and directed our attention to two handlers leading a haltered black Shetland pony in the parade. Its hooves were painted red and blue. The pony had been a symbol of the school since 1932.

Next was the marching band wearing red and white candy striped jacket with white pants, gloves and straw top hats. They had earned the nickname 'the Best Dressed Band in the Land.' I adored the jazz and swing performances they played at school events. It was a trip down memory lane for me and I was enjoying the experience.

We were having a wonderful time watching each of the floats pass with coeds on board throwing candy to the crowd. Each sorority had partnered with a fraternity to build a float. This year's theme was 'Rolling out the Red Carpet.' One float was a miniature replica of Tara from *Gone with the Wind*. Scarlett O'Hara attired in her Twelve Oaks picnic dress and straw hat stood arm in arm with Rhett Butler and waved at the crowd.

"I love it!" I shouted jumping up and down, clapping my hands in time with the fight song.

"Gosh, is that Katherine?" Sarah gasped.

It most certainly was. Riding on top of the back seat of a gold convertible Ford Mustang was Katherine. A banner across both sides of the car read 'Katherine Gold, Distinguished Alumnae and Homecoming Queen, Class of 1990.'

"Please," Olivia sneered with contempt. "She looks ridiculous."

The mustang briefly stopped and Katherine stood up in the back seat alternating kisses to the applauding crowd and doing her best rendition of a Miss America wave. Her dark spray tan was complemented by her gold sequin pageant gown and elbow length white satin gloves. More than one star struck man received an elbow to the ribs from his wife or girlfriend.

"This is worse than *Toddlers and Tiaras*. I'm heading to Bubba's for a chicken biscuit," Olivia shouted over the noise. "I've heard about Bubba's on Food Network. I'm not missing out on an opportunity to eat their world famous chicken."

"We just ate," Cassandra reminded her hungry friend.

"I don't define swallowing food as fast as you can to get away from Holly as eating," Olivia retaliated. "It didn't even take the edge off my appetite."

"You're going to have to marry a farmer to keep you supplied with food day in and day out. I've never seen someone eat so much and stay so tiny," she remarked.

Olivia ignored her commentary and returned shortly with a bag of chicken and biscuits. Together we crossed Hill Crest Avenue and headed towards Bishop Boulevard. Everywhere we looked there were red and blue tents with students handing out plates laden with BBQ, hamburgers and hotdogs.

"This is much different from a Tennessee tailgate party," Sarah observed.

"UT has a much larger student body. Neyland Stadium can hold up to one hundred thousand. This stadium is much smaller with seating for thirty-four thousand."

"I'm so used to *Rocky Top*. So this is how the elite tailgate with a jazz band and cocktails," she said with a hint of irony in her voice.

"I love a good tailgating party and this has been top notch," Cassandra stated. We continued to tour the campus and ended up seated around the fountain in front of Dallas Hall. We were enjoying the clear blue skies that graced the day. It was a picture perfect moment with good friends, beautiful weather, gorgeous surroundings and fun festivities. Little did I know our picture-perfect moment would be short lived!

EIGHT

I was so excited to attend my first game in the new Gerald J. Ford Stadium on campus. We walked past the Doak Walker Plaza named for our most famous football player and Heisman Trophy winner.

"This has been such fun. I love game day festivities, don't you?" Sarah asked as we approached the large iron gates.

"Tickets please," a tall gentleman said as he extended his hand.

"Could you please direct us to the skybox? I politely inquired.

"Right this way M'am," he replied as he radioed for an escort. We were taken upstairs to the upper level deck with a beautifully decorated lounge. The panoramic view of the football field was amazing from this vantage point.

"So this is how the rich and famous live," Olivia observed. "I think I could get used to this."

We watched as the Rice players entered the stadium in their navy jerseys and began warming up. Soon after the SMU cheerleaders made a tunnel for the home team to run through. The fans were screaming loudly and you could almost feel the excitement in the air. The hair on my arms stood on end as I heard the band begin the first chords of the fight song.

"May I get you ladies something to drink?" a young lady in uniform approached us. We placed our orders and began exploring the posh skybox.

"Don't you sit in the skybox for the UT games?" Sarah asked Cassandra.

"Sometimes, but I prefer sitting in our regular assigned seats. Nothing beats the excitement of the crowd. It's contagious," Cassandra admitted.

As we watched, the band began a formation at the center of the field in preparation for the National Anthem. The Honor Guard took their spot with the American flag in the center and the Texas state flag and SMU flag flanking either side. Leslie walked up to the microphone and paused as she was introduced. She looked stunning in a beautiful red suit, her long black hair in stark contrast.

"Now ladies and gentlemen, we are proud to have one of our distinguished alumni joining us today from the class of 1990. Please help us welcome to Gerald J. Ford Stadium, Broadway star and Tony award winner Leslie Lane!" the deep voice boomed over the PA system.

As the band struck the first note, Leslie began singing one of the most beautiful renditions I had ever heard of The Star Spangled Banner. Her trained voice sang out clearly as she hit that last high note that so many celebrities and singers often times don't quite reach. She nailed it. The crowd's loud applause was the only acknowledgement she needed for a job well done.

"Her former music professors must be so proud of her," Sarah leaned towards me and yelled over the crowd. "She's marvelous!"

"She really is," I said beaming with pride at my former

roommate. Leslie used to sing scales in our rental house and stretch on a makeshift ballet barre she had installed in our living room. The hours she practiced point proved her dedication to her art.

"I really hope she gets the part in Ron Howard's movie. She is very deserving. She's paid her dues in New York. It's on to Hollywood for her," Cassandra stated wiping the tears from her eyes, touched by Leslie's beautiful performance.

"Here she is now," Sarah squealed and clapped her hands together. "You were wonderful Leslie."

"Congratulations. That was incredible. Your voice gets better all the time," I said warmly to my dear friend.

"Thanks Amelia and Sarah. You are both too kind." It was obvious she was touched by our compliments.

"They are speaking the truth. I feel like I'm in the presence of greatness," Olivia said warmly shaking her hand.

Wow, I had not heard Olivia give someone such high marks before. Music can have a powerful effect on people.

"Let's get some champagne for Miss Lane," Cassandra motioned to the server. "I'd like to toast your impending success in Hollywood." The server passed flutes around for each of us and we raised our glasses in a unified salute.

"To Leslie Lane!" I toasted.

"And to 'the Traveling Tea Ladies,' " Sarah interjected.

"Traveling Tea Ladies?" Leslie paused, "Oh I get the connection to Amelia and the tea room. That sounds like fun. I want to be one too!"

"Today we initiate a new member to our group," I said laughing. We were so glad to share homecoming weekend with her.

"Remind me to give you some autographed playbills and

posters from *Wicked*. I brought them for Charlie and Emma."

"That is so thoughtful of you, Les. They will love them. Thank you," I said.

"I hate to interrupt your little love fest," Katherine cut in with a grimace on her face, her teeth edge-to-edge in an insincere smile. "You two were always each other's one member only fan club."

I had not seen Katherine approach us. She strutted across the skybox still wearing her sash and gold sequin dress.

"Did your face move when you said that or have you had one too many Botox injections?" Olivia lashed out.

"Back down, Liv," I warned her. "Let's not make a scene."

"Yes, let's not make a scene, Annie Oakley," she quipped as she looked Olivia up and down from her boots to her cowgirl hat with an amused look on her face.

"It seems they let just about anyone in here these days," Cassandra said walking forward and shooting daggers at Katherine.

"Ladies, please, behave!" Monica pleaded with the group.

"These two were always so jealous of me, Monica. Jealous of my looks, jealous of my popularity, jealous I always got the lead in the spring production, jealous I ended up with their boyfriends…" Katherine snarled enjoying the pieces of flesh she was trying to tear from my self-esteem.

Leslie lost her temper. "Katherine, I am so tired and belly sick of you thinking the world and everyone in it revolves around you. You have become such a pathetic and hateful person. The sad thing is you are all alone now. Maybe at one time you had the looks; you had the prime parts; and yes even the guys. But it's all fading and now you are only left with the person staring back in the mirror. I truly feel sorry for you!" she concluded shaking all over.

Katherine hauled back and slapped Leslie across the face. You could almost hear a pin drop as everyone in the skybox stopped what they were doing to witness the exchange. Leslie stood in shock with her mouth open, holding her hand to cover the red mark that began to appear on her cheek.

"Come with me Katherine," Monica tugged her sister around. "The press would like to get a picture of you with the SMU president," she reminded her as she quickly led her away. Monica glanced back over her shoulder with worry and concern written all over her face.

"Are you alright?" I asked pulling Leslie's hand away from her face to survey the injury. Her eyes filled with tears humiliated at the exchange.

"I'm fine. I swear, that's the *last* time she will get away with treating me like that," Leslie declared.

"Some ice for your face," our efficient server offered. We had not realized that the catering staff had witnessed the entire exchange.

"Thank you very much," Leslie said as she quickly placed the ice pack on her cheek. "I'm so embarrassed that happened. I should have known better than to trade barbs with her, but I couldn't take it anymore. I'm so sick of her over-inflated ego!"

"Don't worry, Leslie honey. I'm sure no one even noticed," Cassandra lied.

"I think she needs a can of whoop–you—know-what opened up on her," Olivia threatened. "She called me Annie Oakley. Who even thinks to say such a thing?" she wondered aloud.

"I would take it as a supreme compliment," I reassured

Olivia. I felt responsible that Katherine had managed to ruin our homecoming festivities. Whatever possessed her to be so mean and so hateful? I suddenly felt bad for Monica trying to contain all her sister's hate that seemed to ooze from every pore of Katherine's body.

"Poor Monica, she was such a nice kid," I shared with the girls. "I hate to see she spends her time managing her sister's career. It can't be an easy job for her."

I remembered her as being very quiet, shy and sweet. The weekends she did visit Katherine, she stayed at the house and we popped popcorn, watched movies and listened to music. Her sister was seldom there. She was very serious and the complete opposite of Katherine. I couldn't imagine spending all day cleaning up after the messes Katherine had created.

Half-time was soon over and Katherine was led away from the skybox to the football field for the presentation. Monica had managed to keep her busy until then with photo ops, autographs and a few magazine interviews.

We watched from our seats in the box as the SMU band performed a selection of jazz standards and a rowdy rendition of *She'll Be Coming Round the Mountain*. They made a center row in their formation for the homecoming court to walk across the field and we watched as the new king and queen were crowned. It brought back old memories of my former days on campus and past homecomings.

"And now ladies, gentlemen and university guests," the announcer's voice boomed, "please welcome the president of Southern Methodist University, R. Gerald Turner, as he presents this year's Distinguished Alumnus Award!"

The crowd politely applauded as the color guard stood

at attention. All eyes were on the field as President Turner walked to the podium.

"We are privileged today to bestow the award of Distinguished Alumnus to one of our graduates who has achieved great distinction as an Emmy Award winning actress, winning five Daytime Emmys during her career. We are proud to call her an ambassador of our school and today we pause to honor one of our own. She won all of our hearts when she earned the title of Homecoming Queen in 1990. We are very proud today to have her come home to take the walk once again to center field escorted by Peruna to receive her award. Please help give a warm Texas welcome to Miss Katherine Gold!"

We watched attentively as Katherine took the arm of the costumed mustang mascot who was wearing red and blue tails for the occasion. She was smiling as President Turner approached her. She bowed her head as he took a rather large tiara from a pillow held by a color guard member and placed it carefully on her head. The tiara bobbed a bit and Katherine quickly grabbed it before it slid off her head and affixed the side combs firmly to prevent another bobble. Katherine beamed her trademark smile to the crowd and began waving to the onlookers who by now were on their feet applauding.

"This looks like a bad rendition of *Carrie*," Olivia quipped.

"I didn't know they gave a tiara for Distinguished Alumnus Award," Cassandra remarked with her arms crossed.

"That was Katherine's idea," Holly commented standing behind us. "She wanted to make a big production of it!" She was smiling and clapping loudly in our ears as Katherine began walking across the field.

"She startled me," Sarah admitted. "Does she always pop up out of the blue like that? It's bizarre," she complained.

Katherine paced the field taking her time and enjoying the moment. She walked from the center line to the end zone and back waving enthusiastically at the crowd. The fans whistled and clapped as she continued her Miss America catwalk strut. The autumn afternoon sun reflected off her sequins and cast a golden light on her heavily made up face. I watched closely with my binoculars I had packed for the game. Her sash fluttered in the breeze and she had to hold onto it and straighten it several times. She was blowing kisses and mouthing the words 'I love you' over and over again to the assembly.

"Oh get on with it already," Olivia grumbled. "I'm having a flashback to when my cousin made me play with beauty pageant Barbie. I would much rather be horseback riding right now. When are we going to Fort Worth?" Olivia whined.

"She's really milking this for all it's worth," Cassandra observed. "I'm not sure I could have walked the entire field and back in those gold stilettos without breaking a heel or sinking into a divet."

The band continued playing and changing formations. They made two lines on either side of Katherine for her grand exit from Ford Stadium. The crowd joined the band and was clapping to the beat.

In mid-strut, Katherine paused. She looked a bit dazed while the crowd continued clapping.

"Is she coming back for another trip around the field?" I wondered aloud. "I thought once was enough but some people need the adoration and glory," I commented watching closely through the lens of the binoculars.

The crowd didn't seem to mind her stopping. The applause got wilder and more frantic. "Katherine, Katherine, Katherine …" they were chanting in unison.

She pivoted and began making her way towards the sidelines. And then suddenly, she was going down onto her knees as if in slow motion. Her eyes were wide and a frantic expression was on her face. She grasped her throat with both hands. An audible gasp was heard through the crowd who watched in disbelief as she sank onto the grassy field.

"What is wrong with Katherine?" Leslie screamed and grabbed my hand. She was sprawled on her back as President Turner signaled for paramedics from the sidelines. Katherine lay motionless, her face a strange blue. Monica Gold ran onto the field and kneeled next to her.

A sickening hush fell across the stadium as everyone watched the scene unfold. The medics arrived and had begun CPR. They administered chest compressions and had placed an oxygen bag over her nose and mouth. We watched in horror as they quickly placed her on a gurney and rolled her off the field to a waiting ambulance in the end zone. Monica was assisted into the vehicle by several police officers.

As the ambulance pulled away, lights and sirens blaring, a murmur rose up in the crowd. Small children were crying and being consoled by their parents, cheerleaders and band members were comforting each other, shaking their heads in disbelief. What had happened?

Leslie and I put our arms around each other, unable to speak. The announcer came back over the intercom and told the sold out crowd there would be a slight delay in the second half of the game and thanked us for our patience. We all silently said prayers that Katherine would be alright.

I couldn't believe what had happened. It seemed like a bad dream. Olivia was right—this was a bad rendition of *Carrie*. What had happened to Katherine?

NINE

"*I* still can't believe it," Cassandra said somberly. We were all sitting in the living room of our suite feeling the shock of yesterday's events. A copy of *The Dallas Morning News* was on the coffee table in front of us. The headline read, "Katherine Gold Dies at SMU Homecoming Game."

The article had pictures of fans crying in despair. There were also pictures of a temporary memorial outside of Ford Stadium with mounds of flowers left by saddened fans. Quotes from her shocked co-stars from *The Rich and the Lost* were in the paper as well as from the executive directors, the Bowman's.

"It says the preliminary coroner's report lists a heart attack as the cause of death," Sarah read blowing her very red nose. "As much as I didn't care for her personality, I feel sorry that this happened in front of an entire stadium full of people," she lamented.

"How are you holding up, Amelia?" Olivia gently inquired. In all honesty, I had hardly slept and spent a few hours crying on the phone to Shane. It was a terrible tragedy.

"I still can't believe it," I replied hoarsely. I was still wearing my robe and slippers. We had decided to order breakfast in. "I feel as though I can hardly catch my breath," I added.

"Here, sit down," Sarah said and patted the couch next

to her. "You need some coffee and a strong shot of whiskey to settle your nerves," she suggested.

"Coffee for now," I conceded. My eyes were swollen slits and my face was splotchy. "As much as I detested her behavior, I still loved her. She was a big part of my history," I shared with the girls.

"Grab the remote and turn up the volume," Cassandra ordered Olivia. "They are running a script along the bottom of the local news about Katherine."

We listened as the news reporter spoke stoically into the camera. "She was pronounced dead on arrival at Medical City Dallas. Police have not ruled out foul play," the reporter stated.

The news footage showed Chief of Police, Bob Whittaker, speaking to a throng of reporters shoving microphones into his face. "Until a determination is made by the coroner's office, we cannot rule out foul play in the death of Miss Gold. Therefore we are treating this investigation as a possible homicide. At this time, there will be no questions taken from the press. We would appreciate anyone with information pertaining to Miss Gold's death to please contact the Dallas police department immediately," he concluded.

"Foul play?" Olivia asked bewildered. "I don't know what they think they are going to find out from her autopsy. It looked to me like her collapse was caused by a heart attack."

"There must be some reason they are investigating this as a potential homicide. They must have a reason to suspect it wasn't a heart attack," I thought aloud.

"It's simple. She was a celebrity and they are giving the investigation the star treatment. You saw the paparazzi swarming around the chief. This is as big as Anna Nicole

Smith's bizarre death," Cassandra interjected. Her cell phone interrupted her thought and she excused herself to take the call outside on the terrace. When she returned her face was extremely pale.

"What's wrong?" I asked as I jumped up from the couch. I knew my friend well. She wasn't one to be easily upset. Something major was going on.

"I just got off the phone with the Bowman's. Needless to say everyone in the cast and crew is terribly upset and in shock. Katherine had already filmed her final scenes for the show and the footage is being edited now. Of course they have not shared publically her contract was not being renewed," she paused and took a deep breath as she turned in my direction.

"Spit it out, Cassandra. What has you so shaken up?" I said. The hair on the back of my neck was standing on end. I knew something was terribly wrong.

"Amelia, the police are asking if anyone had a motive to kill Katherine. She had been receiving death threats in her fan mail. Monica had tried to cover it up, but the producers felt it was serious enough to contact the FBI due to the hostile nature of the letters," she divulged.

"I for one wanted to toss her around by her hair. She tends to have that effect on people," Olivia admitted standing defiantly with her hands on her hips.

"Hush your mouth, Olivia. You shouldn't speak ill of the dead," Sarah said sternly.

"All I'm saying, Sarah, is that I can see why she didn't have a lot of fans. If her behavior this weekend was any indication of how she normally acted, she could have made enemies with any number of people," she said defensively obviously irritated with Sarah's admonishment.

"She has a huge fan base now," Cassandra claimed. "You can't turn on the TV without a story running on Katherine. *The Rich and the Lost* is running a marathon of Katherine's storyline over the last twenty years. The public is clamoring for everything they can get their hands on about her."

"She's much more famous now than when she was living. Remember how the public became obsessed after Michael Jackson died? Every gossip rag and entertainment show will run this story as the headline for the next month. Mark my word, she's much more famous dead than alive," Olivia ranted.

"It's ironic that she is being martyred as the sweet and innocent 'girl next door' who made it big. Every celebrity interviewed so far as some wonderful story to share about Katherine. It couldn't be further from the truth," I declared feeling a bit guilty as I shared my true feelings.

The hotel phone rang out sharply, startling all of us. Sarah hurried over to answer it.

"Hello. Yes this is Mrs. Spencer's Room. Who is calling? Yes, one moment," she said seriously and handed the phone to me while keeping the receiver covered. "It's a detective from the Dallas police asking for you."

"This is Amelia Spencer," I spoke up.

"Mrs. Spencer, I'm Detective Matt Lincoln from the Dallas Metropolitan Police Department. Would it be possible for you to come down to the station to answer some questions regarding our investigation of the Katherine Gold case?" he politely requested.

"I don't understand. I'd be happy to help in any way I can, but I don't see how I can shed any light on your investigation," I told him.

"I understand you were Miss Gold's college roommate as well as a Miss Leslie Lane," the detective remarked.

"Yes, but I had not seen Katherine in almost twenty years," I said.

"You may be able to provide some details that will point us in the right direction," he persisted. "By the way, do you have any idea of how to reach Miss Lane? We would like for her to come to the station as well."

My mind began whirring as I tried to fathom why the police would want to speak to both Leslie and myself. Were *we* under suspicion? Surely not, I quickly convinced myself. This was routine in any investigation. They were trying to get a base line background on Katherine, I reassured myself.

"I can call Leslie and ask her to meet us. I believe she is still in town," I quickly replied.

"When can I expect you?" he urged not so subtly.

"I will get dressed and be there as soon as I can. Thank you," I said and hung up the phone.

"Who was that?" Olivia asked with a puzzled look on her face.

"I think Amelia needs a lawyer," Cassandra announced.

"Oh no, I don't think so," I quickly answered. "The detective would like Leslie and me to answer some questions about Katherine."

"What kind of questions?" Olivia interjected. "I watch *Law and Order*. I think Cassandra is right. You'd better hire an attorney," she advised.

"Look girls, I know you mean well. I didn't have anything to do with Katherine's death so I don't have anything to hide. If I can help the Dallas police with their investigation, I'm willing to do it," I said stubbornly. I started to head towards the bathroom to shower and change.

"Listen to us," Sarah pleaded. "If for any reason the detective starts to make you feel uncomfortable, you stop talking and ask for an attorney. Promise me!"

"I will. I promise. Everyone, stop overreacting!" I laughed at their protective advice. "I've got to call Leslie and have her meet me at the station."

"I will have the driver pick her up on our way," Cassandra informed me.

"*Our* way?" I challenged her.

"Yes, we are all going!" Olivia pronounced and arched her left eyebrow daring me to defy her. I knew better than to argue with this stubborn red head. I also knew I could use the extra support right now. I was still terribly shaken.

Cassandra called Leslie and spoke briefly to her while I showered. Leslie was in Dallas and due to fly out tomorrow. Cassandra got the name of her hotel and made arrangements to pick her up.

An hour later we were all dressed and riding to Leslie's hotel, a few blocks away. She was standing at the front entrance and met our car.

"Leslie, how are you holding up?" I asked as I gave her a long hug.

"Not so good. I still cannot believe Katherine is gone," she said and dabbed her eyes with a tissue.

"You should think about staying with us tonight," Sarah offered. "We have plenty of room and I don't think you need to be alone right now."

"I agree with Sarah," Olivia concurred.

"I would love to spend more time with you, Les. The girls are right, you shouldn't be alone," I implored her.

"They are right. I will phone your hotel and have my driver pick up your belongings while we are at the police station. We insist," Cassandra persuaded her.

"I don't want to be any trouble," Leslie protested as she shook her head and the tears began flowing.

"Darling, it's no trouble," Cassandra said and leaned forward in the seat. "Would you please swing back by Miss Lane's hotel after you drop us off?" she politely requested our driver. "I would like to pick up her belongings and take them to our suite at the Adolphus."

"Yes M'am Mrs. Reynolds," he answered.

"Leslie, I will tell you what I told Amelia. If for any reason you become uncomfortable with the line of questioning from the detective, stop talking and ask for a lawyer. I have our attorney from Reynolds's already on his way," Cassandra advised.

"Why did you do that?" I questioned.

"Amelia, they are treating this investigation as a possible homicide. That means they are looking for potential suspects and I am not going to see you or Leslie implicated in this witch hunt!" Cassandra declared emphatically. "I have also called Shane and he will be flying into Dallas this afternoon. He agreed with me about an attorney."

"Is that why he hasn't answered his cell phone this morning? When did you two hatch this scheme?" I couldn't believe they decided this without asking me. I didn't know whether to be irritated or relieved. I could honestly use his comforting presence right now.

"While you were getting your shower. Don't be upset with me Amelia. You need to be smart right now," she urged. I didn't have any time to respond as we were pulling in front of the police station. We piled out of the town car and found our way to the front desk.

"Detective Lincoln is expecting us," I told the officer sitting behind the front desk. "Amelia Spencer and Leslie Lane," I announced.

"Mrs. Spencer, Miss Lane, I'm Detective Matt Lincoln," a confident voice announced. I turned as a tall muscular man in his mid-thirties approached our group. He wore a navy pin striped suit and looked as though he belonged on the pages of *Gentlemen's Quarterly Magazine.* He had a strong chiseled chin and offered a wide smile. He shook both of our hands firmly and looked around the group for further introductions.

"Detective Lincoln, these are my friends who are in town with me for the weekend. Cassandra Reynolds, Sarah Mc-Caffrey and Olivia Rivers," I said making introductions.

"Ladies," he said as he shook each of their hands and made eye contact with each of them in turn. His thick dark hair was clean cut and contrasted with his white even teeth. Yeah, this guy could have been cast as a leading man in any film. He had the looks, the confidence and the build for an action movie star but he was pleasantly unassuming.

"Detective Lincoln," Olivia batted her eyes up at him and smiled coyly, "so nice to meet you."

"Can I get you something to drink while I talk with Mrs. Spencer and Miss Lane?" he offered everyone.

"Oh, I think we'll be fine," Cassandra was quick to speak up, not falling for his smooth Texan accent. "We'll be waiting right here."

"If you'll follow me," he stated as we walked down the hallway. We left the threesome behind to make themselves at home in some very uncomfortable looking molded chairs.

He led us to a brightly lit room with a small gray metal table and four matching chairs. The walls were industrial light green cinderblock. He gestured for us to take a seat. The metal chairs were so cold that I could see the goose bumps coming up on my arms.

"Ok. Let's begin," he said turning on a video camera in the corner of the room on a tripod. "I am recording this interview with Amelia Spencer and Leslie Lane with their permission, correct ladies?"

"Yes," I stated flatly. This was much more official than I thought it would be. I felt a lump form in my throat as he began the interview.

"Mrs. Spencer, how long did you know the deceased, Miss Gold?"

"I met Katherine at freshmen orientation in 1986. We were assigned as roommates," I spoke up and tried to ignore the camera. Detective Lincoln began jotting notes on a yellow legal pad.

"Hmm. And would you say this was an amicable living arrangement?"

"Yes, I would say so. Yes, very amicable," I responded. Why were the palms of my hands suddenly sweaty? This tiny room was making me claustrophobic.

"And Miss Lane, how long have you known Miss Gold?" he continued.

"We met our freshman year in improvisational class," she sat up and answered.

"And you became roommates?"

"Yes, our junior year," she replied.

"And the three of you were sorority sisters?" he probed.

He had done his homework. I wondered where he was getting his information.

"Yes we were," I said and watched him make another note. He began flipping through a folder sitting on the table in front of him. He stopped when he found the document he was searching for.

"Who is Jett Rollins?" he surprised me.

"Why do you want to know about Jett?" Leslie demanded.

"For one, you two were both seen at a recent cocktail party arguing with the deceased and the argument involved a Mr. Rollins, correct?" He leaned forward, staring me straight in the eyes, watching for my reaction.

"Jett was my college boyfriend," I answered nervously.

"Weren't you engaged at one time?" he asked point blank.

"I don't see the significance of your question," I protested.

"Just answer the question. Were you engaged to Mr. Rollins?"

"Yes, we were briefly engaged," I conceded. I could feel the heat rising off my body as I began to sweat. I felt as though I had done something terribly wrong from the accusatory tone in his line of questioning.

"And who broke off the engagement?" he continued grilling me.

"What does that matter? That was twenty years ago. They didn't get married. Broken engagements happen all the time," Leslie countered.

"Oh, it matters. It matters very much in this investigation," Detective Lincoln insinuated.

"Amelia, don't say another word. This interview is over. We would like to see our attorney," Leslie demanded.

Detective Lincoln spread his hands in a gesture of innocence. "Look ladies, I'm simply trying to get the facts straight."

"What you are trying to do is imply that a broken engagement from twenty years ago has something to do with Katherine's death," I construed. He was going to learn I would not be so easy to manipulate. "Drop the innocent good cop act."

"I'm giving you a chance to clear yourself in this investigation. You were both seen arguing with the deceased the night before her death and again in the skybox just before she walked onto the field. You both have motives for wanting to see Katherine Gold dead," he surmised and slammed his pencil down on his legal pad.

"All right, I'll cooperate with you if it will help end this Spanish Inquisition. I called off the engagement to Jett," I admitted. I was shaking with anger, incensed with this cop.

"What was the reason the engagement ended?" he pried.

"Amelia, be quiet!" Leslie warned as she grabbed my wrist.

"It's obvious he already knows. Someone has told him. I want him to know my side of things," I said calmly to her. "I called off the engagement because I found Jett and Katherine in bed together," I divulged sitting up straight and smoothing the front of my shirt. I felt totally humiliated admitting this to a total stranger, but I would never let him know that. The shame was not mine. It was Jett and Katherine's.

"What happened when you found them together?" he continued probing.

"What do you think happened?" I replied sarcastically. "I didn't make a pot of tea and sit down and chat with them.

I walked out the door and left," I quipped. What did he expect me to do?

"Did you attack Mr. Rollins or Miss Gold when you confronted them?" he speculated looking up from his notes to gauge my response.

"No! Of course I didn't attack them!"

"Did you damage Miss Gold's car when you left your house?" he alleged. His line of questioning was becoming more bizarre. Where was he getting that idea from?

"Damage her car? Why would I do something like that?"

"Did you flee the US and go to England after finding them together?"

"I had plans to leave for England to study abroad, something I had planned for almost a year. It was a coincidence that I found them together and left for England the next day," I explained, trying my best not to sound overly defensive. He was irritating me and the gloves were now off. I was ready to fight!

"And you didn't damage Miss Gold's car that evening before you left Dallas?" he persisted and threw an eight by ten picture of Katherine's 1990 car onto the table. I looked down at the picture and saw the words "Die Whore" on the driver's side door. He looked closely at me as I was examining the photo.

"I had nothing to do with this. I didn't even know about it," I reiterated and began shaking, upset at his accusation that I would react in such a crude way.

"Katherine had a lot of enemies on campus," Leslie claimed. "She slept around quite a bit and didn't have many friends as a result of her trysts."

"I'm glad you brought that up. Did Katherine sleep with

any of the men you dated in college? Is it possible you were the one who spray painted this threat on her car?" he asked turning the tables on Leslie.

"No, I was with Amelia at the Gamma Phi house. We were having a going away party for her and I ended up spending the night there. I would have to think of who was also there that night. I recall there were about fifteen girls."

"Was Holly Smith one of them?" he guessed. So he had spoken with Holly. No wonder why he had so much background information. I'm sure Holly had shared all the glory days with Katherine back at the Gamma Phi Beta house. She would be a great source of information, especially if it somehow managed to create attention for her favorite sorority.

"Holly was there," Leslie recalled.

"Did you know about Miss Gold's car?" he turned towards me.

"No, I left for the airport first thing in the morning. I took a taxi," I reported.

"And when did you see Miss Gold next?" he continued.

"Friday night at the Meadow's Museum cocktail party," I tersely answered.

"You and one of your friends were overheard saying you would like to toss her around by her hair. Would you mind explaining that comment?" he quoted from a document in his folder.

"Boy, you've been putting in the overtime on this case, haven't you detective?" Leslie scoffed. "There must be a lot of pressure coming from the boys at the top to solve this high profile case. Look, anyone who knows Amelia would know she wouldn't hurt a fly."

But you would, wouldn't you?" he suddenly flipped on Leslie. "You were involved in an altercation with the deceased at the football game. She actually struck you in the face, correct?" He read from his report.

"Yes she did. That doesn't make me a violent person. That makes HER a violent person," Leslie refuted.

"And what led up to this exchange between you two?" he quipped back.

"You would have to know Katherine to understand how she could antagonize people," Leslie said angrily.

"You two were quite competitive during your college years, yes?" he continued unrelenting.

"How so?" Leslie questioned getting more irritated by the second. She pushed her dark hair from her eyes and exhaled loudly.

"Let's see. You were both theatre majors, she got the lead in the spring production and you didn't," he read mechanically with no emotion in his voice.

"Leslie won the Bob Hope award," I pointed out. It was a prestigious award named after the famous comedian who was kidnapped as a prank by the SMU student body and brought to a pep rally in the 1940's. The theatre on campus was named in his honor.

"Mrs. Spencer, please allow Miss Lane to answer her own questions," he warned me. He turned his attention back to Leslie and began again. "Isn't it true you are auditioning for a part in Ron Howard's next movie?"

"Yes, but how did you know that?" Leslie replied. I had to give Detective Lincoln an A plus for doing his homework.

"Wasn't Miss Gold also auditioning for the same part?"

My mouth went dry and I looked over at Leslie to see if

she had known. Her expression revealed that this news came as a total surprise to her.

"If she were auditioning for the part, no one informed me of that," she insisted.

"Were either of you aware Miss Gold had been receiving death threats?" he revealed and paused to scratch his chin.

"I haven't talked to Katherine, written Katherine, or seen Katherine until this weekend, so the answer is no. I wasn't aware she was receiving death threats," I decreed. I hoped that was clear enough for "Deputy Dog."

"And you Miss Lane? Were you aware?"

"I haven't seen Katherine since the Daytime Emmys last year," Leslie admitted.

"But you are in Los Angeles a lot for work?" he emphasized.

"I do work in LA, but I currently live in New York." Leslie was starting to look tired.

"When you saw Miss Gold at the Emmys last year, did you speak to her?" he persisted.

"I try to avoid her as much as possible," Leslie chuckled. "We may travel in the same circles, but we have very little in common," she stressed.

"Are you sure you have very little in common?" he said mockingly. "What about Trenton Sparks? Didn't you two have Trenton Sparks in common?"

For those of you who have been living under a rock for the last decade, Trenton Sparks is an up and coming Hollywood heart throb who was nominated last year for an Academy Award for his portrayal of a wounded WWII soldier in *American Glory Fighters*. He began his career as a classically trained singer on Broadway and had gradually transitioned to the big screen. Trenton was a 'man's man' and had wooed many a leading lady over the years.

"Trenton and I were together for a while," Leslie said fidgeting in her chair.

"What happened?" the police detective asked point blank.

"We drifted apart. He was in LA, I was in New York. It was a bicoastal relationship that ran its course," she said non-chalantly.

"So Katherine Gold had nothing to do with the breakup of your relationship?"

"No, we called it quits before he began dating her," she claimed crossing her arms and looking defiantly at the tall officer.

"And when would you say that relationship ended?" he said cynically.

"Do you want an exact date and time?" she shot back.

Approximate will be fine," he shrugged and uncrossed his legs. He pushed away from the table and placed his hands behind his head and stretched a bit.

"Around March, I would guess," Leslie said hesitantly.

"Around March? Explain this to me…" he said and slid a copy of *People Magazine* across the table. It was dated January of last year. Spread across the double page story was a beaming Katherine with Trenton Sparks on her arm, posing for pictures in front of a chic LA hotspot. The title was 'Trenton Goes for Gold.'

"They were introduced at a party my agent, Rick Jones, was throwing. He asked Katherine to show Trenton around LA," Leslie explained.

"Show her around LA?" he smirked. "Is that what they call it these days?" Detective Lincoln was obviously enjoying himself at Leslie's expense. "When we you aware they were actually dating," he persisted.

Leslie's face contorted slightly and her lower lip began to tremble. "I knew something was wrong right after he left for LA. I just didn't know what was wrong. I guessed he was adjusting to his new lifestyle. I didn't know until much later there was someone else."

Leslie had never shared this with me about Trenton. It's easy to let time go by and not catch up with old friends with a busy work and family schedule. I suddenly felt terrible that I had not been there for Leslie during her break up with Trenton. I was the one person who could have understood the betrayal I'm sure she felt. She had been there for me.

Looking back to last spring, I remembered talking with Leslie on the phone and she had sounded low. When I asked what was wrong, she assured me everything was fine and quickly changed the subject. She was always so strong and independent. I assumed she was fine. I should have paid closer attention but instead began telling her about our decision to sell the business.

I'm sure Trenton, like Jett, was just another conquest for Katherine. Their relationship had been over for a while. Pictures of Conrad Ryan, the much younger 'boy toy,' had been plastered all over the gossip magazines and TV shows for a few months. Was he just another publicity stunt or was he a real relationship? Who would ever really know?

"Did you confront Katherine about the affair?" the detective demanded.

"No, I was in New York. I read about it like everyone else. Trenton and I parted ways—*civilly*," she added with emphasis.

The interview room door was opened by another officer. "Chief wants to see you. Their attorney is here," he told Lincoln.

"Ladies, it's been a pleasure. Please don't leave town and I will need to get your contact information before you leave the station," he requested. He smiled and rose from the table.

Cassandra walked in accompanied by a somber looking gentleman in his mid-fifties. His curly gray hair, tortoise shell frame glasses, and serious charcoal grey three piece suit screamed Harvard Law.

"Amelia, Leslie, this is Thomas Simpson, our lead attorney at Reynolds's," Cassandra said making introductions all around.

"Ladies, take a seat. The DA is still waiting for the coroner's report. At this time, there is no physical reason to believe there has been foul play, but because of the serious nature of her death and the threats the deceased was receiving, they are treating this as a potential homicide," he recited. He paused, removed his glasses, cleaned them on his pocket handkerchief and took his time.

"Ladies, I need to know where both of you were at the time of death. I want you to tell me EVERYTHING that went on the night before. The DA has a witness who reported an argument between Miss Gold and Amelia, not to mention the altercation in the skybox."

He looked at me with concern. I began feeling the room spin. We were now suspects on a very short list. We had a history, we had a motive, and we had been seen with Katherine right before she died. Someone was setting me up!

TEN

*W*e were back in our suite at the Adolphus. Mr. Simpson had decided the best course of action was to wait to hear a definitive cause of death from the coroner. If Katherine had died from natural causes, there would be no need to worry about a suspect list. In the meantime, we were reconstructing a timeline for him of what had transpired at the cocktail party and at the game.

"I want details; who you were with, what was said, when you saw Katherine, everything," Mr. Simpson requested.

"That shouldn't be difficult," Olivia joked. "The 'praying mantis' walked in, the paparazzi went wild, she got nasty, what's new?"

"Olivia, cut the wisecracks!" Cassandra admonished her. "Thomas, please ignore her. Humor is her way of diffusing the situation."

"Need I remind you, Miss Rivers, that you were overheard by several of the catering staff members threatening Miss Gold? That remark could end up putting you at the top of a short list of suspects," Mr. Simpson stressed by clearing his throat for emphasis.

"I never met the woman before in my life!" Olivia said defensively. "I was simply reacting to what she had said to Amelia."

"Crimes of passion are not usually premeditated. The perpetrator is reacting to a set of circumstances or events. You would be surprised how many murders were committed under those conditions," Mr. Simpson pointed out.

"Yeah, remember when the woman ran over her husband three times with her Mercedes Benz when she found out he was cheating?" Sarah interjected. "Her defense was temporary insanity when she saw him with his mistress."

"I find that hard to believe. Three times and she didn't know what she was doing? Give me a break!" Olivia remarked.

"Ladies, let's focus on the cocktail party," Cassandra reminded everyone.

There was a quick knock on the door. Olivia ran to open it and Shane entered our suite. I happily got up from the sofa and rushed towards him, throwing my arms around his neck for a much needed embrace. We stood there holding each other, oblivious to everyone else in the room.

"I'm so glad you're here! You are a sight for sore eyes," I whispered inhaling his clean aftershave. Just having him here made the situation less frightening.

"Shane, let me introduce you to Thomas Simpson," Cassandra spoke up as Shane and I parted. "He's been our head legal advisor at Reynolds's for the last fifteen years. I trust him explicitly to handle the most delicate legal aspects of our personal and business dealings," she reassured him.

"Mr. Simpson, thank you," Shane said shaking his hand. "I am grateful to know Amelia will have counsel in dealing with this investigation."

"Shane would you like something to drink?" Sarah asked motioning him to sit down. "Maybe some coffee or iced tea?"

"More like a gin and tonic, I'm betting!" Olivia stated.

"Actually a strong drink would be good about now. Anyone care to join me?"

While the men got down to business and discussed strategy, Leslie and I stepped outside on the terrace for some fresh air. "I can't believe this has happened, Amelia," she cried as she looked out at the Dallas skyline. "One minute we're exchanging our usual barbed remarks and the next minute Katherine is dead!" She began crying and shaking her head, covering her face with her hands.

"I know, I know," I empathized and wrapped my arm around her shoulders. "This has been surreal. Can you think of anyone who would have wanted to hurt Katherine?"

"I know she had a reputation for being difficult, but I can't imagine a good enough reason to kill someone," Leslie speculated.

"What about this thing with Trenton? Why didn't you tell me, Les?"

"I was humiliated, embarrassed and it was the same song and dance, just a different boyfriend. I knew better than to allow my agent to introduce the two of them. It was my own dumb fault!" she admitted. She was visibly angry. She had balled her fists at her side and was speaking through clenched teeth. I hated to see her go through the pain all over again.

"And then for the cherry on top, to find out from the detective that Katherine was being considered for the same movie role. I had no idea. I was told I had first right of refusal," she snapped.

"Maybe Detective Lincoln was setting you up to see your reaction," I said rather hopefully trying to defuse her anger.

"Yes maybe he was and that is exactly why I don't want either of you talking to him again without me being present," Mr. Simpson warned as he joined us out on the terrace. "I would have never allowed you to answer his questions. Shane filled me in on your past relationship with Miss Gold. Amelia you had a motive. It's as simple as that."

"I may have been upset with Katherine, but I would never hurt her," I retorted.

"That may be true, but the police don't see it in the same light. Infidelity is the number one cause of homicides by women in the US," Mr. Simpson declared and took a sip of his highball.

"But that was twenty years ago! I am happily married and have moved on," I vehemently objected. What was going on here? Was I really going to have to dredge all this up again?

"Miss Lane had motive as well. She also ended a relationship recently because of Miss Gold. And the potential of losing a movie part gives you a double motive, I'm afraid," he pointed out.

"Do you think I did it? If you do, I don't want you representing me!" Leslie shouted as she looked sternly at Mr. Simpson.

"Defense attorneys don't care if their client is guilty or innocent. It's irrelevant to me," he admitted and shrugged his shoulders.

"But it's relevant to me! You will try harder to defend me if you believe in my innocence in the first place," she retaliated.

She was right about that point. I have heard defense attorneys will created a solid defense whether or not their client was innocent. It would seem to me, knowing their client is innocent without a shadow of a doubt would make someone easier to represent.

"Mr. Simpson, I know you are just doing your job. But Leslie was with me in the skybox when Katherine died. She couldn't have killed her," I acknowledged.

"Do you have witnesses who can verify that fact?" Simpson challenged.

"Yes, of course. Olivia, Sarah and Cassandra were there with us as well as all the VIP's SMU hosted that day."

"I want you both to think of everyone you saw there. Who you were introduced to, who did you speak with, everyone! This is vitally important to your case," Mr. Simpson emphasized.

Case? I had hoped it wouldn't get that far.

Shane joined us out on the terrace, a worried expression across his handsome face. "When will you hear something from the coroner's office?" he asked Simpson.

"Tomorrow morning at the earliest, we should have a preliminary cause of death as well as the results of a rudimentary toxicology screening. If we are lucky, the coroner will find out she had an enlarged heart, heart disease or something along those lines," he informed us.

"I think the coroner will find she didn't have a heart at all," Olivia spoke up as she stood by the open French doors.

"Stop that Olivia," Sarah requested and swatted her on the arm. Despite her best efforts, she couldn't help but laugh at the remark.

We all got a bit tickled. Yes, it was tacky and inappropriate, but we needed to relieve some of the built up tension we were all feeling.

"Here's my cell phone number and please feel free to call

me at any time if you think of anything that will help your case," Mr. Simpson told us and turned to take his leave.

"Thank you, Thomas," Cassandra said and kissed him on the cheek.

"Yes, thank you Mr. Simpson," Shane said and shook his hand profusely. "I think we will all sleep better knowing we have such esteemed representation."

Did Shane really think I would sleep? That was the last thing on my mind. I needed to think. Think about who would want to hurt Katherine. Think about my innocence and how I could prove it. Think about my kids and family. Kids! I had not even thought to ask Shane who was watching Emma and Charlie.

As Cassandra ushered Mr. Simpson from the suite the rest of us sat down, emotionally worn out from the day's events.

"Shane, how are Emma and Charlie? Who's watching them while you are here?" I quickly asked.

"Aunt Alice agreed to stay as long as she is needed. She thought it would be a wonderful opportunity to spoil her favorite great niece and nephew," Shane said reassuringly.

"Thank goodness for Aunt Alice," I reaffirmed and sighed deeply. She had been a God send this week with her help in the tea room and now with the children. We were lucky to have such a strong support team within our family.

"Speaking of Aunt Alice and the kids, I'm going to give them a call and let them know all is well and I arrived safely," Shane added.

"Tell them I will call before bedtime and tuck them in for the night. Give Aunt Alice my love," I requested.

"I've got to make a list of people who had an ax to grind

with Katherine," I stated and walked inside to grab a pen and paper.

"Why don't I order room service while you guys work on that?" Cassandra volunteered.

"Put me down for a T-bone steak , garlic mashed potatoes, a side salad with ranch dressing, and a large slice of chocolate silk pie," Olivia requested reading from the room service menu. "Oh and some dinner rolls with butter."

"Anything else, 'Jabba the Hut?'" Cassandra teased.

"I'll take an order of fajitas if anyone wants to share them with me," Sarah suggested trying to make things easy.

"Amelia, Leslie? What about you two?" Cassandra reminded us.

"I don't have much of an appetite right now, but thanks anyway. I need ibuprofen and a good night's sleep. Maybe some herbal tea and a few crackers," I answered. I was very worried about what we had reviewed with Mr. Simpson. His comments were rolling around in my head.

"Leslie?" Cassandra turned towards her.

"Unlike Amelia, I eat when I am stressed. Order for me what you are getting. I'm not the least bit particular," she smiled and sat down next to me.

"When Shane is off the phone, I'll check with him and then call room service," Cassandra reported. She seemed glad to stay busy tonight. We were all a bit jumpy and nervous after our long day at the police station and strategizing with Mr. Simpson.

"All right. Let's think who was at the cocktail party, who spoke to Katherine, who had a past with her and who she might have seen at homecoming," I listed. I was ready to get down to business.

"Monica," Leslie stated.

"Monica?" I asked surprised. Why would she even consider her? She was always quiet and sweet.

"Yes, Monica. She had motive. She was Katherine's sister, always in her shadow, always cleaning up her messes, never leading her own life," Leslie pointed out.

"OK. Monica. We'll put her name down," I agreed. Leslie was right. Monica was with Katherine in the skybox and most likely with her during her walk to the football field. She had been orchestrating interviews with the paparazzi when we last saw her. No doubt she was on the sidelines right before Katherine died.

"Anyone else?"

"Jett," Leslie replied.

"Jett? Why Jett?" I couldn't believe she would even suggest him.

"Jett was at the cocktail party. Remember he came up and told Katherine to back off?" she recalled.

Yes he had told Katherine to back off and he had been very apologetic about the way things had turned out. Maybe he was regretting what he did more than I knew. But Jett? Ridiculous! He had Laura now and the twins. Why would he put his family in jeopardy over something that happened twenty years ago?

"I don't remember seeing Jett at the game," I thought aloud.

"You don't remember seeing him in the skybox, but no doubt he was at the game. He didn't come to Dallas just to attend a cocktail party, I'm sure!" Olivia interjected.

"Olivia's right," Leslie persisted. She had crossed her arms and began nodding her head in agreement. Her green cat eyes narrowed, deep in thought. "Anyone at that game could have access to the field when Katherine was getting her award," she pointed out.

"The Jett I knew would not be capable of hurting someone," I spoke up in his defense.

"The Jett you knew would never have cheated on you with Katherine, but he did," Cassandra spoke up placing a hand on my shoulder for emphasis. "Let's face it, Amelia. How well did you actually know Jett?"

That was a good question. At one time, I would have told anyone I knew him almost as well as I knew myself. The day I found him in bed with Katherine, I realized I didn't know him at all. Maybe he was capable of something as vicious as murder, but we were all getting ahead of ourselves.

"We haven't even heard back from the coroner's office yet, so why are we assuming she was murdered?" I cautioned the group.

"For starters, the police are suspecting foul play for some reason," Sarah reasoned. "They don't usually do that unless there is some evidence. Maybe the hospital uncovered something." She sat down next to me and started twisting her brunette hair.

Sarah was right. Detective Lincoln wouldn't jeopardize his case by jumping the gun before the coroner's report unless there was evidence supporting a possible murder. This was not just a 'high profile' death. They were taking extra precautions because they must have evidence suggesting Katherine's death was not by natural causes. I would have to go to the station in the morning and ask Detective Lincoln myself what was going on. In the meantime, we would continue to work on the suspect list.

"Emma, Charlie and Aunt Alice send their love," Shane told me giving me a brief update of their activities. "Aunt Alice said not to worry about the tea room. She has everything under control and she's having a ball." He came in and took a seat around the dining room table. How are you coming along with the list?" he asked glancing sideways at the names. "Monica and Jett?"

"Monica is Katherine's younger sister, who is basically her 'slave-in-waiting,'" Olivia informed him. "Her joy in life is cleaning up after her sister's illicit love affairs and dealing with the paparazzi. It's a miserable existence I'm sure," she concluded and sat down on the arm of the sofa.

"Why Jett?" Shane asked and looked over at me for an explanation.

"Jett confronted Katherine at the cocktail party two nights ago when she started giving Amelia a hard time," Olivia enjoyed telling him. "Don't worry, Shane. I took care of her," she gloated.

"That's why you may end up as a possible suspect in all of this if Katherine's death is ruled a homicide," Cassandra glared at Olivia.

"Sounds like I missed quite a party," Shane joked to the group of ladies standing around him. "What exactly happened or should I even ask?"

We all took our turns, giving our best imitation of Katherine's entrance to the party, her vampy posing for the paparazzi and her rude behavior.

"And then I told Amelia I would have thrown her out by her 'Goldilocks' if I had caught her in bed with my fiancée and according to the police, one of the catering crew overheard my comment," Olivia sheepishly admitted.

"Who didn't hear you, Olivia?" Cassandra rebuked her. "You know how loud you get after you've been nipping the tequila."

Olivia got red in the face and continued to defend herself. "Look, it was only two shots of some very fine tequila, I might add. It was nothing like my night of mechanical bull riding. I was under control," she snapped back at Cassandra. She got up and began adjusting her jeans. "When's dinner getting here?" she impatiently asked, ready to change the subject.

"That's our Olivia," Cassandra decreed, "a slave to her appetite!"

"I love the dynamics of your friendships. You're so funny," Leslie laughed.

"Just like *Steel Magnolias* on steroids. Cassandra is Shirley McClaine's character Wheezer!" Olivia joked.

"You take that back right now," Cassandra demanded and chased Olivia around the room. "Take that back this instant! I'll show you Wheezer!" She began throwing pillows at Olivia. It was good for everyone to let off a little steam.

"Ladies, ladies, keep it down before the hotel calls security and then we really will be in trouble!" Shane teased. He shook his head, laughing at the scene in front of him.

Little did Shane know the trouble that tomorrow would bring to "The Traveling Tea Ladies." Today was just a warm up for what lay ahead.

ELEVEN

I managed to get a few hours of uninterrupted sleep before I woke up with my mental list of suspects. I decided to sneak out of bed and let Shane sleep in while I ordered some hot tea. Luckily, the Adolphus had a nice selection of loose teas to choose from. After deciding on some chocolate croissants, fresh fruit salad, herb and goat cheese omelets, a nice pot of English breakfast tea and a strong pot of Kenyan coffee, I was ready to take a shower. I quickly dressed before room service arrived.

I heard a quiet knock on the door and ushered the attendant inside. With quiet efficiency, he set the dining room table for six and dropped off the morning paper. I tipped him and thanked him as I closed the door.

"Good morning, Amelia!" Leslie said as she wiped the sleep from her eyes. "How did you sleep?" She stretched and yawned, her arms extended above her head.

"I slept some. I thought maybe after a nice breakfast we might take a trip over to the campus and do a little investigation of our own," I suggested.

"Did I hear someone say breakfast?" Olivia excitedly asked as she rushed into the room.

"Morning, Liv. How did you sleep? I asked. She tied the belt of her green silk robe and took a seat.

"I slept pretty well though I sleep better at home with the sounds of the river outside my window," she replied and began eyeballing the croissants. I knew I better get everyone else up before she ate more than her fair share.

"Hold it right there, Olivia Rivers," Cassandra warned pointing at her. "Step away from the croissants and you won't get hurt!" She was already dressed in a snappy black sweater set with hounds tooth checked pants. She was such a classic right down to her large pearl earrings.

"Good morning everyone!" Sarah said as she came into the room wearing a kimono style silk robe in bright turquoise. It had a brilliant ceremonial dragon embroidered across the back.

I went around the table and poured everyone their choice of coffee or tea. Some habits die hard. I am used to waiting on guests and it was good to stay busy today. It helped to steady my nerves.

The chocolate croissants were decadent and I enjoyed every scrumptious bite. They were almost as good as 'La Madeleine's,' a French patisserie near campus I had loved to patronize. We all were rather quiet as we ate our omelets. Finally after a second cup of coffee, we began to revive and were ready to plan our strategy.

"If we have to be stuck in Dallas for a day or two, you might as well do some shopping and sightseeing and make the best of it," I suggested to the table of ladies. Shane had just joined us, his hair still damp from his shower.

"We are here to support you. We can shop and sightsee another time," Cassandra pointed out and looked around the table for confirmation.

"I agree with Cassandra," Sarah quietly said. "I wouldn't

feel right about shopping while you were being investigated in a murder!"

"How can we help, Amelia?" Olivia asked taking another bite of her second croissant. "Anyone have an idea?" She licked her fingers and continued eating undeterred.

"I've been thinking we should return to the scene of the crime and talk with anyone who might have seen anything during the half-time show," I shared.

"Good idea, Amelia," Shane agreed. "First, I'm going to go by the police station and talk with Detective Lincoln and see if the coroner's report is in. Ladies, if you'll excuse me," he said politely.

"There's no need, Shane," Cassandra stated showing him the front page of *The Dallas Morning News*. "The preliminary autopsy report is in," she read aloud.

The headline read, "Golden Girl Dies by Apparent Poisoning." A grotesque picture of Katherine on a gurney was next to the caption. An oxygen mask was on her face, her eyes were closed, her skin slightly blue, her golden mane disheveled.

"Poisoned?" Olivia asked incredulously. "Are you sure?"

Shane read on: "The initial toxicology reports showed a lethal level of an unknown poison in her bloodstream. It will be a few more days before the specific poison is identified. Police are looking for the source and delivery method." He shook his head in disbelief. We were all rather somber as this new information sank in.

"Who would do that to her?" Leslie demanded, her anger barely contained in her trembling voice. "What a terrible way to die!"

"Maybe it was something she ate? Did anyone see her

eating while she was in the skybox?" I began replaying Katherine's entrance into the VIP suite over in my mind. We were standing next to the buffet when she came into the room.

"I don't remember her eating anything," Olivia remarked.

"You would know," Cassandra said in all seriousness, "since you planted yourself right next to the buffet most of the first half of the game."

"She's right," Sarah affirmed. "Olivia, did Katherine even get that close to where you were standing?"

"Not after I made that Botox remark. I moved back over by the oyster bar. Katherine never came close to me after that," Olivia recalled.

"What Botox remark? Never mind! I don't want to know," Shane said shaking his head at Olivia. "You were never one to mince words."

"Maybe she was poisoned by a drink?" Sarah speculated. "Did anyone see her drink anything in the skybox?" she asked excitedly.

"No I don't remember her holding a drink," Leslie murmured. "As I recall, she was being interviewed most of the time. She was also busy being introduced to all the Texas big wigs, politicians and oil men."

"Maybe someone handed her a bottle of water on the way to the field? Maybe it was spiked with poison?" I deduced.

We all began nodding our heads, deep in thought, trying to figure out the mode of delivery.

"Who would know if she had something to drink after she left the skybox?" Shane asked.

"The one person I can think of is her sister, Monica Gold," I quickly replied. Maybe Leslie was right after all about Monica. She should be at the top of the suspect list.

She had the most to gain from Katherine's death. I could think of two possible scenarios; a substantial inheritance and freedom from her controlling narcissistic sister.

"Girls we've got to find out where Monica is staying and talk with her. Maybe she saw something that could clear our names," I announced.

"Hurry and get dressed, Olivia!" Cassandra snapped, "We've got to find Monica and fast before she leaves town."

"It will only take me a minute to throw on my boots," Olivia yelled as she dashed from the table, her green robe flowing behind her.

"Wait for me too," Sarah called over her shoulder. "I can't go out in a kimono."

"I will try to make a few phone calls to LA to see if anyone knows what hotel Katherine and Monica were booked for the weekend. I'll be right back," Cassandra added and grabbed her phone out of her black patent leather clutch.

"I hope Cassandra can find Monica before she flies out," I said beginning to get anxious. What if she did leave town? How would we be able to find out who she had seen with Katherine? We had to clear our names.

"I hope we're not too late," Leslie said running her fingers through her long black hair. She had started to get dark circles under her eyes. She looked as though she had not slept much the past two days.

"I don't think Monica will leave without the coroner releasing Katherine's body. I think you should be able to track her down," Shane hoped. He was still reading the paper, studying it for clues of what might have happened.

"Did you know they just announced a special tribute planned for Katherine at next month's Emmys? She will be receiving a lifetime achievement award, posthumous of course," he read.

"I'm going to flip on the TV while we are waiting for Olivia and Sarah. I want to see the local weather forecast. October can be warm one day and cool the next in Dallas," I recalled and rose from the table. The local news was plastering pictures of Katherine from the cocktail party and her collapse on the field. They even had grisly footage of her in a body bag. I quickly turned off the broadcast. It was just too much for me right now.

"She's bigger now than when she was alive," Leslie remarked.

"Yes she is," Cassandra agreed coming through the terrace doors. "My Hollywood contacts just told me that Andrew Morton is writing a tell-all book about her life. Rumor has it as a million dollar book deal."

"Isn't he the same author who wrote about Princess Diana?" Shane asked surprised by the news.

"Yes as well as Madonna and Tom Cruise," Olivia blurted out as she came into the room wearing a smart brown bolero jacket, dark denim dress jeans and ankle-high chocolate brown boots.

"When did you become the official celebrity gossip queen?" Cassandra said in a belittling tone. She crossed her arms waiting for Olivia's response.

"I guess in order to keep up with you and all your 'Hollyweird' friends I have been doing a little celebrity reading."

"Like what?" Cassandra asked in total disbelief.

"I don't know. *People Magazine*, occasionally *US Weekly*," she confessed.

"You of all people? I don't believe it!" Cassandra challenged.

"I'm ready," Sarah announced coming into the room wearing black leggings, a long matching tunic and ebony beret.

"What are you, some character from *The Pink Panther* dressed for espionage?" Olivia teased her. At least she and Cassandra had temporarily stopped their banter.

"I figured I should dress the part. You never know when you'll need to blend in," Sarah said seriously with a pert nod of her head.

"I don't call that blending in since berets are a French fashion staple, but OK," Olivia conceded.

Sarah put on a very large pair of sunglasses. She did look as though she were moonlighting for the CIA or undercover agency. I went over and wrapped my arms about her neck and let out a deep laugh.

"No one can say we are dull, that's for sure!" We were an odd group.

"The car is waiting and I have Monica's hotel information," Cassandra interrupted. "Let's hit it girls. Shane, what's your plan?"

"I'm meeting with Thomas Simpson at the station with Detective Lincoln. I want more details about the autopsy and to check on leads," he replied. He was wearing a navy blue cable knit sweater over a blue button down. He was calm and collected, but had a determined glint in his eye I knew very well.

"Do you really think Detective Lincoln will share privileged information with you?" I asked him as I straightened his collar and smoothed the front of his sweater.

"I don't know, but I can't sit around and go stir crazy. I've got to try," he said and gave me a quick kiss as the elevator doors opened. "I will call you and tell you what I find out.

Ladies, be careful today. You don't want to go poking your noses where they don't belong," he warned us. Truer words could not have been spoken.

TWELVE

*W*e drove to the Crescent Hotel, a European style beauty in the center of Dallas. It was every bit as lavish as the Adolphus, but it had a much different feel. It was among the most upscale hotels in the country.

We stepped into the lavishly appointed lobby and waited in the lounge for Monica to join us. Cassandra had phoned ahead to let her know we were on our way. She had seemed very receptive to our impromptu visit.

"Monica, I'm so sorry for your loss," I lamented and squeezed her tight.

"Thank you, Amelia. Thank you," she mumbled as though in a daze. Her face was drawn and void of color. She was wearing a simple navy blue pair of slacks with a white button down blouse. She gently wiped her nose with a tissue and gestured for us to join her at a nearby table.

"Monica, I would like to introduce my friends from Dogwood Cove. Olivia Rivers, Cassandra Reynolds and Sarah McCaffrey," I announced.

"Hello, so nice to meet all of you," she said shaking hands with everyone.

"I'm so sorry, Monica," Leslie told her as she gave her a heartfelt hug. Monica began crying and took off her glasses. She dabbed her eyes and tried to compose herself.

"I can't believe Katherine is gone! She was all the family I had and I feel so lost without her. I can't tell you how much I appreciate your support. Katherine didn't have many friends and it would mean so much to her to know you were here with me right now," she acknowledged.

"Do you have any idea what happened?" I asked hoping to get down to the facts.

"No, she was fine. We did interviews and she posed for the paparazzi the entire walk down to the field. She was fine," she insisted. Monica became overwhelmed with tears as she recounted Katherine's final moments. We all began to tear up as we watched helplessly.

"Monica, honey," Leslie said in a soothing tone. "The paper this morning is reporting she was poisoned. Do you have any idea how she could have been exposed to poison?"

"She seemed OK. We ate breakfast together and she never once said anything about feeling sick or tired. In fact, we both ordered the same thing. She was very excited to receive her award," she shared with us.

"Could someone have handed her bottled water or something to drink that could have been laced with a toxin?" I asked. "Maybe it happened on the way to the field at half-time?"

"She was offered something to drink, but didn't want to mess up her makeup," she recalled. "She knew it was a big photo op for her and she was very particular about her appearance."

So it was not her breakfast. Monica and Katherine had ordered the same thing. She had not had anything to eat or drink in the skybox or on the way to the field. Then how was the poison administered? I was perplexed. Nothing was adding up unless Monica was lying to us.

"Monica, dear, I don't mean to upset you with what I'm about to suggest, but it has to be mentioned. Was Katherine having problems at work?" Cassandra inquired holding Monica's hands in a show of support.

Monica began wringing her tissue. She looked very uncomfortable with Cassandra's question. She began to speak, her voice quivery. "Katherine was not the easiest person to get along with and she didn't make many friends on set, at least not many women." She was visibly trembling and Sarah got up to get her a glass of water.

"Here you go, sweetie," Sarah said and patted her shoulders. "Drink this and try to calm down." Monica looked up appreciatively at Sarah and managed to continue.

"Katherine was a vital woman ... she had many lovers," she revealed and cleared her throat taking a sip of water. "Some of the men were married and some were co-workers boyfriends. She just didn't understand the meaning of off limits," she sighed and cast a sideways glance in my direction. She sank down a bit in her chair. I knew then she was aware of what had happened between Jett and Katherine.

"She was receiving some fan mail that at first was critical about Katherine's personal life. Then it became increasingly scary with cut up pictures of Katherine re-pasted like a puzzle with images of blood and skulls in the background. It was very disturbing," she recounted.

"How many of these gruesome letters did she receive?" I asked.

"Maybe ten at the most over the last three months. The FBI seized them as part of the investigation," she informed us.

"Could this demented person have been at the homecoming game? Did you notice anyone behaving strangely or following you around?" I persisted hoping she would remember a face or description.

"There was one man in particular among the paparazzi that made some very inappropriate remarks to Katherine," she remembered. "He wasn't someone I recognized from LA. He was at the cocktail party and again at the game. I did my best to try and keep Katherine as far away from him as possible," she assured us.

"What did he look like?" I quickly spoke up, hoping a description might give us a lead.

"Dark brown hair, what sounded like an Italian accent and he was wearing a black baseball cap. He kept screaming at her, calling her a slut and home wrecker," Monica stated.

Olivia averted her eyes and then glanced across the table at me. I could tell she was thinking what we all were at the time. Katherine had wrecked many relationships and had a reputation of being promiscuous. The photographer's comments were mild in comparison to what our sorority sisters had said to her in years past when she had slept with their boyfriends.

"You mentioned you were not familiar with him. Do you have any idea if he was with a specific publication or freelancing?" Sarah spoke up.

"No, I don't have a clue. I told the police about him and they are reviewing the footage from the cocktail party to see if I can spot him in the crowd. We might get lucky and get an ID," she said hopefully.

"Monica dear," Cassandra hesitated, "was there anyone at work who had it out for Katherine? Someone who may have made threats towards her?"

"Well, yes. Like I said, Katherine had a lot of attention from men. Sometimes that caused friction on set when she was involved with one of her co-stars," she divulged. She hesitated and looked anxiously around the table. I guessed she might feel as though she were betraying her sister by sharing her private information.

"We're not here to judge," Sarah spoke up as she took a seat next to her. "We want to help find who did this and bring justice to Katherine. Anything you can think of will help us to help the police," she insisted.

Thanks goodness Sarah had come with us. She seemed to be a stabilizing factor at this moment. I was grateful Olivia was keeping mum at the moment. If I could only read her mind!

"She had recently ended an affair with Bo Bronson on not such a good note," Monica revealed. Bo Bronson? Bo Bronson? I wracked my brain trying to remember who he was.

"Bo Bronson plays Thad on *The Rich and the Lost*," Olivia informed me when she saw the puzzled expression on my face. "He is one of the established characters on the show," she shrugged as though everyone had a plethora of soap opera information they could pull out of their heads like a computer.

"My, Olivia, I had no idea you knew so much about the soaps," Cassandra couldn't help but tease.

"What happened with Bo?" I asked trying my best to ignore the barbs that would fly at any moment between these two jokers.

"He was madly in love with Katherine. It was very intense for a few months until his wife, Sheila, found out about their relationship. She showed up on set and caused quite a scene. They had to stop filming for almost an entire day due to the fall out! Bronson is in the middle of a nasty custody battle and divorce," Monica conceded.

"What happened between Katherine and Bo?" I pushed.

"Bo proposed," Monica added nonchalantly. "By then Katherine was bored with him and had begun to see Conrad. Bo became crazy. He was insanely jealous and said he would ruin Katherine for breaking up his marriage and two timing him. He said she made him look like a fool!" She was twisting her tissue again and seemed agitated. Recalling all the recent events had to have been hard on her.

"How about a pot of chamomile tea to settle our nerves?" I suggested.

"I think that would be wonderful. I'll find someone and place an order," Sarah volunteered.

"She had decided to leave the show because of Bo," Monica declared. "She couldn't deal with his jealousy on set every day."

Cassandra shot me a shrewd look. "Monica, the talk around town is that Katherine's contract wasn't renewed. Is there any truth to this?" she asked in all sincerity.

"Yes and no," she paused and slipped off her glasses. Her eyes were extremely red and swollen. "Sheila Bronson's uncle is one of the producers of the show. Sheila was hell bent on Katherine's head rolling. She insisted on her being fired." She took another sip of water before continuing.

"Katherine was more than happy to leave. She had become fearful of Bo and his temper. She told me he had been following her and had refused to accept their relationship was over. And Sheila had some very powerful friends. She vowed to ruin Katherine's career," Monica detailed.

Wow. It sounded as though the past few months had been horrible for Katherine. She had a scorned wife to deal with and a jealous ex-lover. No wonder she was making plans to return to Dallas. It sounded like she was running away from a nightmare.

"What do you mean Bo was following her?" Olivia spoke up as she leaned across the table, her interest peaked.

"He would park his car outside her house at all hours of the night. There was one incident where he showed up at the same restaurant as Katherine and Conrad. She found out later he had hacked into her cell phone and looked at her calendar and text messages. He made a big scene during their dinner and punched Conrad in the face. It was horrible the way he stalked her," Monica concluded.

"I remember hearing about that. Wasn't Bo arrested for assault and battery?" Olivia remarked.

"Yes and a restraining order was issued by the judge. It was as if he had morphed into a monster! If he couldn't have her, no one would!" Monica said.

"Did you tell this to the Dallas police?" Cassandra spoke up.

"No. I didn't think it had anything to do with her death. I assumed it was a heart attack," she said as her shoulders began shaking. She laid her head against my shoulder and I put my arm around her and held her close. Poor Monica was all alone now.

Sarah returned with our server and a hot pot of chamomile. We spent the next few minutes sipping tea and allowing the hot liquid to coat our throats and our tea cups to warm our hands. We were all quiet thinking about everything Monica had shared.

"How was your relationship with Katherine?" I asked after a lull in the conversation. "I know you acted as her assistant. It must have been difficult to be her sister and also work for her," I pushed knowing this might be my only chance to talk with her. I was willing to nudge her to get my name cleared and Monica was the last one who had seen Katherine alive. She was vulnerable at this moment and might be willing to speak candidly.

"Our relationship had its ups and downs. She could be very trying at times," Monica said taking a long sip of tea. "It wasn't my idea to work for her, but she had a hard time finding an assistant that worked out for more than a few weeks before they got frustrated and quit. She said I was the one person who truly understood her," she related to us as she let out another sob. "I put my college education on hold to help her. Now what will I do?"

"You don't have to figure anything out right now," Cassandra reassured her. "When you are ready, go back to school. Education will open all sorts of doors for you."

"I'm thinking of a career change right now," Sarah shared with her. "A change will do you good too!" She patted her arm and poured her a second cup of tea.

"Don't get me wrong. I must sound ungrateful. I loved my sister but I had not planned on working for her. It was no life for me; answering fan mail, making appointments, booking hotels, airline reservations and dealing with the paparazzi. Some days it was too much!" She pushed her bobbed hair back with both hands and exhaled deeply. "Katherine didn't get it. She told me I should be thanking her for the job. She didn't understand that I felt lost about who I am and what I want for myself. It always has been all about her and I know how awful that must sound! I've been going to a therapist for a while to work out some of my issues," she admitted.

I nodded in agreement. She had devoted her life to Katherine and from what I could tell, life with Katherine had been challenging for her. Monica needed to take some time for herself and figure out her next step.

"How is Conrad holding up?" Leslie asked.

"I haven't spoken with him. He and Katherine called it quits a few weeks ago when she decided to move back to Dallas. Neither of them were any good at long distance relationships and his career is in LA. He's already moved on to someone else," she casually mentioned.

"Who is it? Jennifer Aniston? Cameron Diaz? Tell us," Olivia asked hanging on the edge of her chair.

"Get a grip Liv," Cassandra chided. "Who cares who Conrad is dating?"

"Was Katherine seeing anyone in Dallas? I inquired.

"I'm not aware of anyone, though she was being secretive about some meetings that were not on her appointment book. If she was seeing someone new, I wasn't aware of it," Monica frowned.

"I want you to know that Leslie and I have been questioned by the Dallas police about Katherine's death," I shared with her.

"You and Leslie? What could they be thinking?" she asked stunned.

"They think Amelia is still heartbroken about Jett Rollins," Olivia blurted, "and Leslie must still be heartbroken over Trenton Sparks."

"That's preposterous!" Monica declared shaking her

head furiously. "You three were so close in college. There is no way you would ever hurt Katherine."

"Thank you for saying that, but as far as I'm concerned, it's all ancient history," I remarked.

Monica and I had shared some good times when she visited her sister. I think we must have watched *Dirty Dancing* at least twenty times. I remembered she had a crush on Patrick Swayze.

"It's definitely ancient history for me too," Leslie added.

The weekends Monica had visited, Leslie and I usually ended up entertaining her while Katherine was out with her latest conquest. We both felt bad she didn't make time for her sister. If Monica had felt slighted, she had never complained.

"You weren't even near Katherine when she collapsed. Why would they suspect you two?" she asked.

"Detective Lincoln is going on motive, I presume. I think it would help the police if you could trace exactly what happened on the sidelines before Katherine collapsed," I strongly suggested to her.

"I've tried to go over everything. I wish I could remember something," she stammered.

"Start with who was near Katherine on the sidelines," Olivia prompted her. "Did you notice anyone suspicious? Maybe someone was out of place or wearing dark sunglasses and a hat?"

We were all wearing sunglasses, Liv!" Cassandra said exasperated. "It was sunny and we are in Texas. No one goes anywhere without their sunglasses in Dallas," Cassandra snorted at her friend's lack of reasoning.

"I thought it might help Monica remember," Olivia said

defensively and crossed her arms and glared at Cassandra.

"What do you remember happening right before Katherine walked onto the field?" Leslie interjected. She fiddled with her teaspoon and finally rested it on the back of her saucer. She seemed to have a lot of nervous energy as we all did.

Monica concentrated and answered, "We stopped and did a short interview with the Fox News affiliate and one with NBC who was televising the game. We stopped at the fifty yard line to wait for Katherine to be announced."

Monica was staring down at the table, tracing patterns on the white linen tablecloth with her index finger. She took another sip of tea. I noticed her hands shook slightly when she brought the teacup to her mouth.

We all sat quietly around the table allowing her time to gather her thoughts. She set her cup down and continued, "I have wracked my brain trying to think of anyone who might have had contact with her. By the time we reached the field, the players were in the locker room, the band was playing and we stood next to the SMU president. I just don't understand how she could have been poisoned. I was with her the entire time. This doesn't make any sense at all!"

She banged her fists on the table and I jumped slightly. She had a right to be frustrated. I was too. She put her head down on the table and began crying again. I couldn't imagine the pain she was feeling.

Sarah rubbed her back in slow circles. "There, there, Monica. Hush. Just breathe deeply," she said as she continued to stroke her back for comfort. Monica gradually lifted her head, dabbed her nose, and thanked Sarah. This had to have been a difficult conversation for her and she looked exhausted.

"Katherine walked out with President Turner and that's when he announced the award and made the presentation," Leslie recounted the events.

"And then he placed the tiara on her head," Olivia joined her as she pantomimed lifting an imaginary tiara in the air and placing it on. "She then walked across the field and waved to the crowd and then she collapsed. So what happened?"

"How could she have been poisoned?" Monica sobbed. "I was there the whole time. We ate together, stood together. I stood right next to her during the interviews. I don't know how this could have happened." Monica looked exhausted and shell shocked.

"Amelia, why don't I stay here with Monica and keep her company. She has a lot going on right now," Sarah suggested.

"You don't have to Sarah. I'm really fine," Monica insisted as she blew her nose.

"Sweetheart, you've been through an ordeal," Cassandra reminded her in her Southern drawl. "Sarah is right. You shouldn't be alone right now."

"It's decided," Sarah said with determination. "Let's go back to your room and I can run a nice bubble bath for you."

"Sarah, you have your cell phone on you, right?" I affirmed. "We'll head over to campus and catch up with you two later."

"Come on Monica," Sarah said and assisted her to the elevator.

"What do you think of all of this, Amelia?" Cassandra asked. "She came up with a whole list of new suspects; Bo Bronson, Sheila Bronson, the Italian photographer, and whoever sent the threatening letters."

"And don't forget the police suspect you, Jett and me," Leslie added with a sarcastic laugh.

"And then there are those mysterious appointments Katherine kept from her sister. Maybe there was a new man in her life?" Cassandra insinuated.

"You're forgetting the one person who had the most access to Katherine and motive as well," Olivia pointed out to us, "Monica!"

"That poor child could hardly get through a sentence without breaking down. There is no way she did it," Cassandra scoffed.

"Guilty people cry too. They do it all the time on *Cold Case,*" Olivia acknowledged with authority in her voice.

"Oh good grief, Liv! You and your TV shows," Cassandra declared and threw her hands up in the air in a show of exasperation.

"Hey, she ate with her, stood with her, she had opportunity. She was going to a therapist because she was unhappy working for Katherine. Maybe she cracked!" Olivia ascertained.

"I don't know what to think. The Monica I knew twenty years ago would not have been capable of murder, but people change. Maybe she figured she couldn't quit working for Katherine and was desperate. As much as I love Monica, I can't rule her out as a suspect," Leslie admitted.

I felt awful we were even suspecting her, but Olivia was right! She had a motive, her alibi was Katherine and it was the classic *Cinderella* story of the oppressed sister being overlooked and treated poorly. But *Cinderella* didn't murder her step sisters.

"Do you really suspect Monica?" I asked the group. "If

that's the case, we shouldn't leave Sarah here with her," I pointed out.

"I honestly don't believe she had anything to do with it and I consider myself an excellent judge of character," Cassandra spoke up. "Sarah's fine. There is nothing to worry about. She has her phone, she can call us if she needs us and I'm certain once Monica takes a bath and relaxes, she will be sleeping for a good long while. She's safe, Amelia."

"I don't think Monica would hurt anyone. I just needed to hear someone else agree with me," I said.

"I'll call the driver to bring the car around," Cassandra said.

We rose together and headed toward the entrance of the Crescent Hotel. Maybe our trip to Ford Stadium would uncover more clues.

THIRTEEN

We were all quiet during the short drive to the SMU campus.

"I just can't wrap my brain around Monica doing something like that," Leslie thought aloud and frowned. "Poisoning is so violent. The Monica I knew wasn't violent. She was a great kid."

"Maybe her therapist could shed some light on her mental stability," Cassandra suggested.

"Not happening! The doctor patient confidentiality oath prevents her therapist from talking to the police, let alone one of us," Olivia stated in a robotic tone.

"That's it, I'm cutting you off from your legal shows!" Cassandra scoffed.

"Cassandra, would it change your mind about Monica if you found out she was Katherine's beneficiary? She mentioned there was no other family. More than likely she was the sole beneficiary since Katherine had no children and had never been married," Olivia reminded her. "Amelia, call Shane and find out what he learned at the station."

"I will after our visit to campus. I want to get there before the maintenance crew leaves for the day," I informed her.

Our driver pulled up to the curb outside of the Ford Stadium ticket window. We quickly exited the vehicle and

Cassandra gave the driver instructions to wait for our return.

"This is the main gate to the stadium. I hope it's open," I said as I pushed against the towering iron door. "Drat, it's locked!"

"Look for the delivery entrance. That's where you'll find an open gate," Olivia simply stated as if everyone should know that kernel of knowledge.

"Who are you, *Cagney or Lacey?*" Cassandra ribbed her. "I had no idea you were such a good investigator!"

"Give me a little credit," she sighed and lightly swatted Cassandra's arm.

"Looks like you were right. The delivery gate is open," I pointed out.

No one was in sight so we let ourselves in. The driveway opened up onto the field. I felt so small and insignificant as I walked towards the sidelines and looked at the towering stadium walls and rows of empty seats encircling us. We could see the skybox from this vantage point.

"We were right up there," I pointed.

"And Katherine stood right here at the fifty yard line," Olivia recalled and placed her feet on the painted white hatch marks on the turf. "She walked straight out," she said and held her elbow out as if being escorted. "She stood here while he announced the award and then ..."

"President Turner placed the tiara on her head," Cassandra cut in, squarely positioning an imaginary tiara on Olivia's head.

"She turned, walked to her right, I'm waving, I'm waving..." Olivia motioned looking up and smiling at the skybox.

"And then she grabbed her throat and fell on her knees," Cassandra finished.

"Yes and then the paramedics rushed in from over there," Leslie joined in pointing to the tarmac. "They checked Katherine, put her on the gurney and rushed her to the hospital," she recalled.

"We're missing something. What are we missing?" I wracked my brain trying to recall a key clue. Something wasn't right. I couldn't figure out what it was. My thoughts were interrupted when my phone rang. It was Shane.

"Shane, how did it go with Detective Lincoln?" I asked hopefully.

"That's why I'm calling. Where are you?" he quickly asked.

"I'm at the football stadium. We were going over Katherine's final moments," I replied. Suddenly, I realized what wasn't adding up! "Shane, do you still have this morning's paper?" I blurted.

"Yes, I brought it with me. Why do you ask?"

"I want you to look at Katherine's picture and tell me what you see," I requested.

"I don't understand. What are you looking for?"

"Please. Just describe to me what you see in the picture," I pleaded.

"Katherine is on the gurney, her eyes are closed. She's wearing an oxygen mask. I don't get it," he complained.

"Is she wearing anything else?" I quickly interrupted.

"Like what, clothes?" he asked confused.

"No, a tiara. Does she have a tiara on in her picture?" I reminded him, the excitement rising in my voice.

"No she does not. I'm still not understanding, Amelia!" he said in a frustrated tone.

"Shane, see if Detective Lincoln has the tiara listed with

her personal effects," I requested a bit impatiently.

"Want to tell me why?" he insisted.

"She collapsed right after President Turner placed the tiara on her head. It could have been the vehicle for introducing the poison," I deduced rather proud of myself.

"A tiara, really Amelia?" he belittled me. "Ridiculous!"

"Ask him Shane and call me back when you find out. I'm going to ask the maintenance crew if they found her tiara on the field. Call me right away," I snapped and hung up. Ridiculous? I think not. I turned toward Olivia.

"Genius, Amelia! If you're right, the poison entered her system when the tiara was placed on her head. It fits the symptoms and collapse," she hugged me impulsively. "Let's find the maintenance office, pronto!"

The four of us retraced our steps to the tarmac and looked around for signs leading to the office. A uniformed worker walked towards us.

"Can I help you ladies?" he offered.

"Yes, Dan, I think you can," I said reading his name badge. "Were you here during the game Saturday?"

"Yes Ma'am. That sure was a sad day. Poor Miss Gold," he lamented.

"We are actually close friends with Katherine. We were her roommates in college and we are helping her sister out with some of her personal effects," Leslie stepped up and tossed her long silky black hair over her shoulder. Dan seemed mesmerized by her.

"Anything I can do to help," he whispered and shyly cast his eyes downward. He looked back up at Leslie and grinned.

"Dan, did you find anything belonging to Katherine? Maybe a shoe, a purse, or maybe a tiara?" she said and gazed wantonly in Dan's eyes. Obviously, Leslie had practiced this move before.

"You know, you're the second person that has come by today asking about a tiara," he spoke up.

"Someone else came by asking about Katherine's tiara?" Olivia asked astonished, her voice rising ever so slightly.

"Yeah, a police woman with the Dallas police department," he informed us.

"Did she give her name or show her badge?" Olivia questioned him with her hands on her hips.

"No, I don't think I remember her showing a badge," Dan recalled.

"Did you find the tiara?" I asked him. I was holding my breath in anticipation of his answer.

"I did. I was on the field and the referee picked it up before the game resumed," he told me.

Great! The police would have the tiara. I pulled out my phone to call Shane and share the good news. He answered on the first ring.

"Shane, the police have the tiara. I just spoke with a maintenance crew member and he found the tiara," I shared with him.

"I'm here with Detective Lincoln. They don't have a tiara," he informed me.

"The police woman who came by picked it up," I stammered.

"What police woman?" Shane asked.

"I don't have her name, but she came out to pick up the tiara from a maintenance worker," I explained.

"Let me talk with Lincoln and I'll call you right back," Shane said.

"Dan, where is the tiara now? Did you give it to the police woman?"

"You know the phone range and I turned my back to answer it. When I turned around, she was gone. I thought that was rather strange!" he remarked.

"Did you give her the tiara?" Olivia asked him getting agitated and tapping the toe of her boot.

"No, I didn't have a chance. She was gone before I turned around," Dan replied defensively.

"Take us to the office right away!" I demanded and slung my handbag over my shoulder, following Dan's long strides as best as I could. My stomach sank and I felt slightly faint. He led us to the maintenance office a short distance from the field. He opened the door and walked over to the main desk.

"Marge, these ladies are here to retrieve Katherine Gold's personal belongings," Dan informed an older woman with leathery skin siting behind the desk. She turned towards us and peered over her reading glasses.

"What tiara, Dan?" she asked with a puzzled expression.

"It was right here this morning," he said and began fumbling between the stacks of invoices and outgoing mail bin.

"I never saw it and I came in around ten o'clock this morning," Marge told him and got up from her chair to help assist in the search. "A tiara, you say, like a crown?" she reiterated.

"Yes a big crown like Miss Universe," Olivia told her. "Katherine was wearing it when she collapsed on the field."

"Such a shame, such a shame," Marge empathized. "She was such a beautiful woman!"

"I can't find it anywhere," Dan turned towards Marge

and shook his head clearly bewildered. "I don't know what could have happened to it."

"I have a pretty good idea," I told the group. "How long did you have your back turned on the police woman, Dan?"

"Maybe three minutes at the most. I had to take a call and then radio a truck. Yeah, three minutes."

"Long enough for her to come behind the desk, grab the tiara and takeoff," I surmised.

"She said she was with the Dallas police," he argued.

"And I'm Paris Hilton," Olivia said off handedly. "You always get the badge number and ID Dan," she reproved him.

"I ... I ... I didn't know, but I didn't give her the crown. She must have taken it," he stammered.

"What did she look like, this police woman?" I questioned him. I was getting the sinking feeling she wasn't affiliated at all with the investigation and we had just lost the key piece of evidence to clear our names.

"She had dark brown hair, glasses, kind of medium height. She was wearing a black suit. That's about all I could tell you," he shrugged.

"If I didn't know any better that almost sounds like Monica Gold" Olivia said suspiciously.

"I'm calling Shane right now," I informed everyone as my phone rang before I had a chance to dial. "Shane, I need to speak to Detective Lincoln right away," I spoke into the phone.

"At your service," Detective Lincoln answered formally with amusement in his voice.

"Oh, I'm sorry, I thought you were Shane," I admitted and placed my hand over my chest, embarrassed by my mistake.

"Shane told me you were on campus talking with a maintenance person who said one of our female officers was out there today," he acknowledged.

"Yes, that's right."

"Did he get her name because I didn't authorize anyone to pick up Miss Gold's belongings at the stadium? Furthermore, we don't have a female officer assisting with this investigation."

"That's what I was afraid you would tell me." There was no police woman. Dan had been duped hook, line and sinker. The evidence had vanished and I was still a suspect.

"Come on over to the station, Mrs. Spencer. I think we need to talk," Lincoln requested.

"Sure. Let me call my attorney and I'll be right over," I told him. Could this day get any worse?

FOURTEEN

Mr. Simpson met me at police headquarters. I sent Cassandra, Olivia and Leslie back to the Adolphus Hotel to relax and have some down time. There was nothing they could do to help me at this point.

Cassandra reassured me she would call and check on Sarah and hopefully all of us could get together for some dinner when I was finished with Detective Lincoln. I hoped I wouldn't be having dinner in "cell block-d" tonight wearing an orange jumpsuit courtesy of the correctional department.

"Amelia, don't answer any questions without my consent," Mr. Simpson implored. "Let's find out exactly what evidence Detective Lincoln has before we get upset and answer questions without thinking, OK?" He patted my arm reassuringly as we were ushered into the same cold, sterile room with the industrial metal table and chairs. Mr. Simpson pulled one out for me and I sat down, waiting to hear my fate. He opened his briefcase and took out a legal pad.

"Mrs. Spencer, Mr. Simpson," the Detective said as he came into the room and shut the door. "Your husband tells me you have an interesting theory as to what may have happened to Miss Gold. I'd like to hear it," he requested. He pulled out the chair directly across from me and sat down.

I looked over at Mr. Simpson and he nodded his approval. "I think Katherine was poisoned by someone who delivered the toxin through her tiara," I said.

"This sounds a bit to me like a bad copycat of the movie, *Miss Congeniality.*" He laughed skeptically, "And conveniently the tiara is nowhere to be found. So I suppose that lets you off the hook," he said mockingly.

"Maybe instead of questioning me, you should be looking for this woman who is impersonating a Dallas police officer. She knew the tiara was a valuable piece of evidence and took the risk of going back to retrieve it!" I retorted.

"You have any more theories up your sleeve, *Kojak?*" He chuckled at this own joke. There's nothing I despise more than a smart aleck. Detective Lincoln fit the bill.

"Have you spoken with Monica Gold recently?" I asked leaning towards him. I was not about to be intimidated by his rude rhetoric.

"We spoke yesterday. Why?" he snapped. He knew I had valuable information. If he wanted me to share it, I'd make him grovel.

"Katherine had a lot of enemies from what I gathered from Monica," I said cryptically.

"Yes, the FBI told me about her fan mail," he said unimpressed.

"Did she tell you about the Italian photographer and the Bronson's?"

"We are working to locate the photographer right now. We were able to ID him. Who are the Bronson's?" he asked surprised. I had him now and I knew it.

"Bo Bronson was Katherine's married co-star whom she began an affair with a few months back," I disclosed to him.

"I thought she was seeing that Conrad kid," Lincoln admitted and scratched his head. Obviously he had not been keeping up with the celebrity gossip.

"According to Monica, that's been over with for a while. She broke up with Bo after she started seeing Conrad, but not before Sheila Bronson, his wife, found out and got her fired from the soap. Apparently she is related to a producer," I told him smugly. I had done my homework and was proud of myself.

"From what I gathered, Miss Gold dated married men as a hobby. So what's the big deal about this Bronson fella?" he said flippantly, though I knew he was obviously interested.

"Bo had begun stalking her. He was even arrested for assault and battery after attacking Conrad at a restaurant. There was a restraining order against him," I recited.

"You've been doing your homework, *Columbo*. That still doesn't let you or your friends off the hook," he said and smiled slyly from the left corner of his mouth.

"Are you charging my client with anything at this time, Detective?" Mr. Simpson demanded. "If not, I am requesting you to stop throwing around your false accusations."

"There were a lot more people interested in hurting Katherine than me," I retaliated. I didn't appreciate his snarky comments.

"Like who?"

"Like Sheila Bronson who was in the middle of a nasty custody fight, Bo Bronson who was being two timed by Katherine, and let's not forget the photographer who was haranguing her. We now have a mystery woman who took the tiara from the campus office this morning. She could very well be your killer."

"Your old boyfriend, Jett, would be another possibility," he redirected.

"Jett had nothing to do with this. If you are interested in looking up alibis for everyone that lost a boyfriend to Katherine or who slept with her, you would have to question just about everyone who attended our class reunion," I quipped.

"Yes, we have been interviewing quite a few of your classmates. They claim you dropped out of sight after Katherine's affair with Jett," he said and leaned back in his chair. He flexed his arms behind his head, a cocky smirk across his face. He was enjoying this! Boy he was working hard to get under my skin, but I was determined not give him the satisfaction.

"That's enough. If you are done, Detective Lincoln, my client and I will be leaving," Mr. Simpson interjected. He opened his briefcase and began packing his notes.

"Look, Detective Lincoln, I didn't do it. Even though Katherine had her flaws, I loved her like a sister," I asserted.

"Even sisters can kill," he said self-righteously.

Was he hinting that Monica Gold was a suspect? My first inclination was based entirely on the Monica I knew from twenty years ago. My knee jerk reaction would be to defend her. I had to keep reminding myself I didn't know Monica as an adult and there were obvious problems between them, enough to require therapy. She also matched the description Dan had given us of the woman impersonating a police officer. I decided to keep my suspicions under my hat for now. I didn't want to implicate her until I knew for certain.

"Yes, that's true but speaking of sisters, I suggest you talk to Monica Gold again. She mentioned Katherine had some appointments she kept quiet from Monica who as you know was her personal assistant. She can also tell you more about Bo and Sheila Bronson. Maybe you should see if they were in town over the weekend," I argued.

I got up and grabbed my purse. I was tired of being treated like a criminal, tired of Detective Lincoln wasting valuable time when he should be looking for the real murderer and emotionally exhausted.

"Mr. Simpson, please remind your client not to leave town until we're finished with this investigation," he stated as he pushed in his chair. He was becoming quite annoying.

"I have two children and a business to run back in Tennessee. I need to get back home as soon as possible. I've already extended my trip and made myself available to answer your questions," I pointed out to him.

Business, my business! I should be packing up the tea room this week! The closing was set for next Friday. I had a lot of work ahead of me. My life had literally been put on hold the moment Katherine Gold had died.

"Please remind your client I can hold her for up to seventy-two hours without charging her with a crime. Her cooperation would be a good show of faith to the court," he intimated and quickly took his exit. I stood there with my mouth hanging open.

"Can he do that?" I asked shocked at the thought of being held that long.

"Yes, he can and yes, he will if you do not cooperate fully. I already informed Shane you may be here a few more days. It would be best to make arrangements for the care of the children," Mr. Simpson recommended as he adjusted his bowtie and grabbed his briefcase from the metal table.

"Amelia," he said as we exited the room, "don't give up

hope. This will be over soon. The police are just doing their job," he told me.

"Doing their job? Doing their job? I don't think harassing me instead of looking for this imposter police woman is doing their job. I practically gave that man a hand written list of who's who and all he can do is make condescending remarks and threaten to hold me!" I shouted as we walked down the hallway.

"I'm sure Detective Lincoln is already following some of your leads. Cooperation goes a long way with the Texas courts," he explained.

I knew the sooner things wrapped up, the sooner I could go home, back to my kids and my life. I had to find that tiara and solve Katherine's murder. I'd have to keep digging for more leads.

"Amelia, sweetheart," Shane said and embraced me as I walked into the waiting room. "Did everything go OK, Thomas?"

"I assured Amelia the more she cooperates with the police, the sooner she can go home. Shane, Amelia, I will remain in town until this matter is resolved," he assured us and extended his hand to Shane. He gave him a firm handshake and patted me on the arm. "Get some rest, Amelia," he said as he headed out the door.

"Yes, rest. That's why I'm here. My lady, your chariot awaits you!" Shane announced made a sweeping motion with his arm toward our car and quickly opened the front door. As I sank into the soft leather seats, I felt some of the tension of the day dissipate.

"Shane, you need to go back home. The kids need one of us there and we've got a lot going on with the closing next week," I objected.

"Not another word, Amelia. You and I are going to have a nice relaxing dinner and we're not talking about anything unpleasant. You need to unwind and relax and I'm here to make sure you do!" he insisted and gave me a kiss on the cheek. He held my hand and smiled encouragingly at me.

"Where's everyone?" I suddenly realized.

"The ladies are shopping at The Galleria Mall. I'm sure it will be a while before they are done," he predicted.

"Is Sarah with them?"

"Yes, they picked her up. Monica decided to stay in for the night. Everyone is occupied and happy. Now it's your turn!" he decreed.

"Shane, I miss the kids so much! I wish I were home. I would give them both the biggest hugs and never let them go. This has become a nightmare," I remarked. I looked out the window at the Dallas skyline.

"Speaking of kids, Aunt Alice is having a ball with them and they both want you to call them right away." He pulled his cell phone from its holder and dialed our home.

"Hello, Charlie?" I squealed.

"Mom, I'm so glad you called. When are you coming home?" he asked with a twinge of sadness in his voice.

"Soon, baby. Real soon! How's football going?"

"I threw two touchdowns yesterday! It was so awesome because the ground was muddy and we were covered in it. John Holston skidded halfway across the field when he caught my pass," he told me.

I could just picture the dirty uniform and cleats waiting for me when I got home. I could also picture his freckled face splattered with mud.

"Have you finished your homework for tomorrow?" I reminded him.

"Yep! I'm helping Aunt Alice make oatmeal raisin cookies. I think these may be my new favorite," he predicted.

I laughed at the thought of my kitchen back home bustling with the activity of baking cookies and the wonderful aromas filling the house.

"Did you finish your library book?"

"I'm working on it. I have to take a test on it tomorrow," he blurted.

"Get it done and don't skip to the last chapter and read the ending," I warned him. I knew my son well enough to know he often tried short cuts when he had other thing he would rather be doing like baking cookies and hanging out in the kitchen with his favorite aunt.

"I love you, Mom. Come home soon," he pleaded.

"I love you too, Charlie. I'll be home as soon as I can. Is Emma nearby?"

"I'm right here, Mom," Emma piped up.

"Hey, Emma!" Gosh it was good to hear her voice. "How is everything going?"

"Good, good. We miss you, though," she reminded me. That was Emma, always so thoughtful.

"Not as much as I miss you guys. Hey, are you getting help with your homework?" I stressed.

"I've got it covered. Nathan has been coming over to help me study," she said.

"Nathan Johnson?" I asked. Oh no. I needed to get home and keep an eye on this situation.

"Yes, Nathan Johnson. Don't worry, Mom. Aunt Alice is making us study in the kitchen. She feeds Nathan dinner and he helps look over my work. He's the smartest kids in my class," she reassured me.

"Yeah and the probably the cutest too," I teased.

"Mom, I don't like him like that. We're just friends, gosh!" she objected.

"I remember saying that about your Dad," I joked.

"When are you coming home?" she cleverly changed the subject.

"Soon. How's Aunt Alice doing?"

"Great. She's a lot of fun. Don't worry, I already washed Charlie's uniform," Emma informed me.

Wow, she was becoming quite responsible. "Thanks Emma. You're something else. I'm so proud of you," I rejoiced.

"Why because I can do a load of laundry?" she joked.

"No because you did it without being asked. There's a difference," I insisted.

"I know, I know! I'm special, right?" She was laughing now.

"You know it, sweetie," I agreed. Gosh, I missed that sweet face and bright smile. "Can you put Aunt Alice on the phone?"

"Sure. Here she is. Love you, Mom!"

"Love you too, Emma. I miss you," I told her and blew her a kiss over the phone.

"Hello, Amelia," Aunt Alice called out in a sing-song rhythm.

"Thank you so much for staying longer." I was glad to know she was there giving the daily stability to the kids.

"There's nowhere I'd rather be. How are you holding up, dear?" she asked in a maternal tone.

"I'm glad Shane is with me, but I think he needs to go home and be with the kids," I admitted.

"We are holding down the fort. You worry about you. I'm enjoying the tea room and the children. It's been fun for me to get back in the restaurant groove again. I have no plans until Christmas so you take care of what you need to do and take your time," she maintained. She was reassuring and generous. Thank goodness for Aunt Alice.

"Thank you! You're a lifesaver. Hopefully we will have this resolved before Christmas!"

"You will be home soon darling, don't worry," she reaffirmed. "I'll save you some oatmeal raisin cookies."

"I doubt there will be any left after Charlie starts eating them," I laughed and smiled at the thought of Charlie putting his hand repeatedly in the cookie jar.

"He reminds me of Shane so much. Shane had quite an appetite at that age," she reminisced.

"He still does," I told her and pictured Shane and Alice baking cookies when he was a young boy. He and Charlie were two peas in a pod.

"We're here," Shane prompted and I looked around, unaware that we had arrived at The Mansion on Turtle Creek, our dinner destination.

"I'm going to have to go, but I will call in the morning. Thank you again, Aunt Alice."

"You and Shane take care and we're doing fine. I will keep you in my prayers," she concluded.

Shane came around to open my door. I needed some quiet time alone with him. I would put off worrying about everything until tomorrow.

FIFTEEN

While everyone slept in, Shane and I stole a quiet moment to share a pot of coffee and some warm cinnamon rolls.

"What did you and Lincoln talk about yesterday? I asked him as I felt the morning sun's rays on my fair Irish skin. I pulled on my cable knit sweater to prevent too much of a good thing knowing my dermatologist would be happy.

"Don't you want to wait a bit before we plunge into all this again?" he suggested.

"Look, we agreed last night not to talk about it, but that was last night. If I'm going to clear my name and get home to my family, I need to figure this out. The police don't seem to be doing such a hot job of it right now," I asserted.

"The police know more than you realize. In fact, the toxicology report should be in today and Lincoln promised to phone Thomas with the specifics on the poison that killed Katherine," he remarked.

"Really? They're sharing information?" I jeered. I couldn't believe Lincoln would discuss the case with a suspect's attorney.

"I think after you called with your lead on the phony police woman, he knows you are actually trying to help," he concluded.

"He didn't act like he appreciated my help yesterday. If anything, he treated me like I was fantasizing about the tiara since it conveniently disappeared," I retorted and took a large bite from my cinnamon roll, taking my frustration out on the gooey confection.

"Cassandra was going to talk to her LA connections yesterday to see if anyone knew where Sheila and Bo Bronson have been over the last few days," Shane reminded me. He picked up the morning paper and began perusing the headlines.

"Let's not wake her up too early. LA people are on the Pacific time zone," I reminded him.

"It looks like we won't need to bother her with that phone call," he said handing me the front page. In big bold letters the headline screamed, "Bronson Kills Wife in Murder-Suicide Sunday."

"Shane, how horrible!" I covered my mouth in astonishment and continued reading the article out loud. "The police said they received a nine-one-one call from one of the children reporting their mom and dad were fighting. Bo Bronson had entered the home with a rifle. Oh, Shane! How could he do that when the children were home?" I cried in disbelief.

"He was obviously disturbed. Those poor kids," Shane agreed and shook his head in amazed silence.

"Monica told us he had been following Katherine and had even hacked into her cell phone. He was charged with assault and battery after he attacked Conrad and Katherine at a restaurant. He was a loose cannon," I shared with him.

"When did all this happen?" Shane asked as he walked out to the terrace and leaned his forearms against the railing.

"It was a few months ago. She had a restraining order

against him," I informed him. "Shane, the article said Sheila and Bo had a divorce hearing on Friday and full custody had been awarded to Sheila. Bo had been issued a contempt charge for disorderly conduct during the divorce hearing and spent twenty-four hours in jail," I recited as I continued reading the article.

"That clearly establishes the Bronson's were nowhere near Dallas on Saturday," Shane deduced. "First Katherine, now Bo Bronson. This is not looking good for *The Rich and the Lost*. They've had two major stars die in one weekend," he said.

"It's good for ratings," Cassandra said as she walked out onto the terrace. She was wearing a baby blue pant suit today and looked chic.

"I guess you heard?" Shane spoke as he walked inside to pour a second cup of coffee.

"It's all over the TV this morning. They already are doing a special program linking Bo and Katherine's deaths. Their relationship had become public toward the end. This is just what the viewer's eat up," Cassandra groaned. She poured herself a cup of coffee and helped herself to a cinnamon roll. "Mmm, these are wonderful! Quick, let's eat them before Olivia wakes up," she joked.

"Did you have a productive shopping trip last night?" I asked hoping they had enjoyed their time at The Galleria. I couldn't bear the thought of my friends coming to Dallas and not seeing all the sights of the city.

"Olivia has officially turned into a shop-a-holic. I think I have created a monster," Cassandra stated.

"What do you mean?" Shane asked bewildered.

"She went crazy in the Prada store. I practically had to

tear her away when they announced the mall was closing," she recounted as she wiped her mouth on a linen napkin.

"Are you talking about *our Olivia?* The one who would rather be 'dead than wear designer?'" Shane quoted.

"Cassandra has helped Olivia tap into her inner-diva," I explained. "She is realizing there's more to life than mucking stalls and baling hay."

"I resent that remark!" Olivia spoke up as she joined us on the terrace. "I thought I smelled cinnamon rolls!" she exclaimed as she stacked two on her plate.

"Good morning, Liv," Shane greeted her and watched with an amused look as she inhaled her breakfast. "Did you sleep well?"

"Yes, but someone was talking in their sleep last night," she complained.

"Who?" I asked.

"Leslie. Something was obviously bothering her. She kept saying she was sorry over and over again," she recalled.

"Hmm, I wonder what could be wrong?" I said moving over to make room for Olivia.

"Did you hear the news this morning?" Cassandra inquired.

"What news? What did I miss?" Olivia demanded becoming excited.

"Bo Bronson murdered his wife and then shot himself Sunday morning," Cassandra stated matter-of-factly.

"Why would he do that?" Olivia exploded.

"I think he was a very unstable person," I spoke up.

"Do you think he was the one sending Katherine those freaky fan letters?" Olivia speculated as she took another bite of her roll.

"It's possible. He definitely was disturbed enough to send them and they started a few months ago about the time she ended it with him," I agreed. "I think I should give Detective Lincoln a call."

"Save your call. He's here," Sarah announced and escorted the tall officer to the terrace.

"Matt," Shane greeted him and shook hands.

"What brings you out so bright and early this October morning? Continuing your witch hunt?" Olivia said curtly.

"Amelia, Don't say a word until I call Thomas," Cassandra warned and began dialing the attorney's number.

"That won't be necessary. I'm not here to question Mrs. Spencer," he assured us.

"Don't believe this slick talker," Olivia sneered in the detective's direction.

"You can call off the firing squad," he said and shot Olivia a spiteful look. "I'm here to share information."

"Share information with him and you'll be sharing a cell with 'Big Bertha,'" Olivia forewarned.

"Liv, it's OK," Shane told her. "Detective Lincoln is just as interested as we are to catch Katherine's killer."

"Why don't we step inside where it's nice and air conditioned," I suggested. It was getting hot on the terrace or maybe the detective's presence got my blood pressure elevated. More than likely it was a combination of the two.

We all gathered around the large glass dining room table and waited for him to speak.

"So what do we owe the pleasure of your company?" Olivia said sardonically.

Lincoln ignored her remark and addressed the rest of us. "You're going to hear this on the news in the next few hours.

We've pinpointed the toxin in Miss Gold's blood stream," he revealed.

"What is it?" Shane asked impatiently.

"Tetradoxin. It's powerful venom that can cause neuro-muscular paralysis within three minutes. Respiratory failure was the cause of death," he told us.

"That explains why she grabbed her throat and made the universal choking sign," Sarah said, her eyes wide in alarm.

"Tetradoxin. I've never heard of it? Where is it found?" I asked Lincoln.

"It's a rare octopus venom," he shared.

"Are you serious? An octopus? I've never heard of an octopus being deadly other than the giant squid from *20,000 Leagues Under the Sea!* To this day, I still can't eat calamari!" Olivia exclaimed.

"You're a nut job," Cassandra mused. "Please excuse my good friend, Detective. Continue!"

"The venom is from a specific octopus, the blue ringed octopus from Australia. Even though it's only the size of a golf ball, one blue-ringed octopus has enough venom to kill twenty-six adult men," he explained.

"How horrible," Sarah gasped. "Remind me not go snorkeling in Australia."

"Your theory, Mrs. Spencer, about the tiara is correct. The coroner found small puncture wounds on either side of Miss Gold's scalp concurrent with the teeth of a comb. He believes this is how the venom was introduced to her blood stream. The scalp is a very vascular area on the body. Death would have happened in a matter of minutes," Lincoln emphasized.

"President Turner was lucky he didn't somehow get exposed to the toxin," Sarah remarked.

"You're absolutely right. The crown was sitting on top of a velvet pillow for the presentation. It appears he didn't have contact with the comb's teeth," he disclosed to us.

"Could he have been the target since this venom is so fatal?" I theorized.

"It's possible. We're not ruling that out. But most likely he would have been collateral damage if he had been exposed. Miss Gold was the recipient of the tiara and therefore the target," he stated.

"Who knew she would be crowned?" Olivia asked.

"I heard it was Katherine's idea to be crowned since she was a past homecoming queen. Didn't Monica say something along those lines?" Cassandra remembered.

"No, it wasn't Monica," I quickly spoke up. Who was it, I wondered? I tried to recall where we had heard Katherine was receiving a crown. Something Olivia had said about the movie *Carrie* was slowly coming back to me. I would mull that tidbit over and figure it out later.

"We still don't know who this mystery woman is who showed up at the campus maintenance office," Cassandra pointed out.

"After we talked with Mrs. Spencer, we interviewed the staff and had a sketch artist work up a drawing. Unfortunately, our main witness had his back to her most of the time, so we are not confident in how accurate the sketch is," the detective told us. He pulled out a black and white drawing of a woman with large glasses and a non-descript face. She looked to be about forty with brown eyes and medium length brunette hair.

"She looks like the woman who waited on me at the perfume counter of Estee Lauder yesterday and about every other woman I saw at the mall," Cassandra remarked.

"That's what worries us. Our witness wasn't very attentive to details," he agreed.

"What's going on?" Leslie asked as she entered the dining room. She was wearing her hair pulled back in a sleek pony tail and had on dark dress jeans and a ruffled green blouse. Her makeup hardly covered the black circles under her eyes.

"Miss Lane," the detective addressed her and politely stood up from his seat.

"Here, Leslie. Have a seat and I'll grab some coffee and breakfast for you if Olivia left any cinnamon rolls for the rest of us," Sarah teased. "Detective, may I get you some coffee as well?"

"Coffee would be great, thank you," he replied.

"Leslie, it's been a busy morning already. Detective Lincoln told us the poison that killed Katherine was from a rare octopus," I updated her.

"What? How is that possible?" she asked as she stirred sweetener into her coffee.

"We believe the combs of her crown were dipped in poisonous venom which entered her blood stream within minutes," Lincoln explained.

"How horrible! Poor Katherine! Why would someone do that?" she asked stunned.

"That was my next question. You had spoken with Miss Gold's sister. Have you been in contact with her today?" he asked us.

"No," Sarah said, alarmed. "I left her around two o'clock in the afternoon. She said she wanted to take a nap and needed some time alone."

"She's not at her hotel," Lincoln stated and took a sip of his coffee. He placed the cup down and continued. "Housekeeping said her things were still there, but her bed had not been slept in. Any idea of where she could have gone?"

"Oh, no! I knew I shouldn't have left her alone!" Sarah cried, as panic rose in her voice. "She was so upset yesterday. She said something about being the only one who understood Katherine."

"I'm sure she is probably busy making Katherine's final arrangements," Cassandra offered and tried to ease Sarah's fear.

"We've run a trace on her cell phone and her GPS monitor is not working. We have no idea where she is," Lincoln reiterated. "I was hoping you could remember some place she used to hang out or someone she might be visiting?" he asked.

"No, I can't think of any specific place, can you Leslie?" I answered and looked to Leslie for confirmation.

"No, she always hung out with us. She's not originally from Dallas," she added.

"If you hear from her, I need to speak with her immediately," he prompted us.

"I guessed you heard about the Bronson's this morning? You can cross them off your list of suspects," I told the officer.

"That is what I wanted to speak with Miss Gold about this morning. The FBI has linked Sheila Bronson's fingerprints to the threatening fan mail."

"What? She must have truly hated her," Sarah declared.

"Bo wasn't the only unstable person in that marriage," Shane commented as he fidgeted in his chair. "This had been a morning of revelations."

"You're still looking for the mystery woman from the sketch as well as the Italian photographer?" I inquired.

"Yes, we've ruled out your old acquaintance, Jett. He was sitting with a group of fraternity brothers during the half-time show and had been with them most of the morning. His alibi is solid," he shared as he gave me a sideways glance. "Again, if you speak to Miss Gold, please have her call me right away."

"Of course, thank you," Shane said and stood up from the table.

"Ladies, if you'll excuse me. Olivia," he said and nodded in her direction, "a pleasure as always." He left our suite as the door shut loudly behind him.

"That man gives me the creeps," Olivia remarked and rubbed her arms as though she felt a chill.

"More like goose bumps, I think!" Cassandra noticed. "If I didn't know better, I would think Detective Lincoln has found himself a woman strong enough to spar with him."

"Cassandra, I wouldn't have anything to do with him if he were the last man on the planet," Olivia shrieked.

"I think thou dost protest too much," Cassandra mused. "He definitely made a point of saying goodbye to you."

"I noticed that too!" Sarah joined in. She was wearing a pair of black pencil leg Capri pants with black ballet flat and a scoop neck sweater. She reminded me of Aubrey Hepburn, cute as a button.

"Stay out of this, Sarah!" Olivia warned.

"He did make a point of saying your name," Sarah defended her position.

"Here we go again!" Shane laughed. "Has anyone seen Leslie?" he wondered.

"I think she's on the terrace," Sarah spotted her.

I walked over to the French doors and saw Leslie standing with her hands on the railing, her shoulders moved up and down as though she were privately crying. I had detected something had been bothering her the last few days. Maybe she would tell me why she was out of sorts.

"Leslie are you OK?" I asked as I walked out to stand beside her. She was looking at downtown Dallas as tears streamed down her face. Something was terribly wrong with her. I put my arms around her shoulders for support and held here while she sobbed, obviously wracked with pain.

"There's something I never told you," she admitted between gulps of air. "You know when you left for England, I stayed behind at the apartment for the summer?" she paused and swallowed.

"Yes, I remember."

"Amelia, I don't know how to say this except to just say it and get it out," she cried and dabbed her eyes.

"Tell me! What in the world is so wrong?"

"Katherine found out she was pregnant two weeks after you left for London," she said and looked up at me. "The baby may have been Jett's."

"Baby? What baby?" Had I heard it correctly? Katherine had been pregnant? I didn't remember hearing anything about a pregnancy.

Leslie continued to watch my face and spoke slowly. "Katherine had a baby. She found out she was pregnant right after graduation. No one else knew about it and I didn't want to add any more pain after your broken engagement," she confessed.

I turned away from her. Katherine had been pregnant.

Jett could be the father. I gripped the railing until my knuckles turned white.

"Amelia, are you OK?" Leslie's concern was genuine.

"Wow, I wasn't expecting to hear that. Did Jett know about the baby?"

"I honestly don't know. Katherine and I were not on speaking terms when she left to move back west with her aunt. It wasn't too long after that she landed the part on the soap," Leslie explained and continued to cry.

I shook my head, pulled a tissue from my pocket and wiped my eyes. "I didn't know things would get worse. What happened to the baby? Did she have it?"

Leslie shrugged her shoulders. "I don't know. I really don't know. Like I said, we didn't speak for a long time. Maybe Monica would know," she concluded.

Monica. Yes, Monica would know. And if Katherine had a child, that child needed to know that he or she had just lost their mother.

"We've got to get hold of Monica right away and find out about the baby," I shouted and grabbed Leslie's hand. We rushed inside to the living room of our suite.

"Amelia, sweetheart, what's wrong?" Cassandra asked as she rose from the love seat.

"Can we take the car back to the Crescent Hotel?" I quickly requested.

"Yes, of course. Is everything all right?" Cassandra asked bewildered.

"Katherine was pregnant and Monica may be the only one who knows what happened to the baby," I told the group. "We've got to talk with Monica and find out what she knows," I told them all.

"When did this happen?" Olivia asked first. "Did I miss something?"

"Pregnant, when?" Shane asked.

"Right after graduation," I told them as I gathered up my handbag.

"Right after she slept with Jett," Olivia surmised.

"Yes, I didn't tell Amelia. She was already too hurt," Leslie explained.

"That was probably for the best, don't you think Amelia?" Sarah said and walked towards me. She held my hand as a show of compassion. Sarah was always the peacemaker.

"But Monica is missing. The police are looking for her now," Olivia pointed out.

"Olivia has a point. The police probably have someone at the hotel waiting for her. What do you hope to gain by talking with her about a baby?" Shane asked as he looked at me sympathetically.

"I'm thinking that child has a right to know what happened to his or her mother. Think about Charlie and Emma," I looked directly at Shane as he nodded his head in agreement. "This is not about Jett," I looked around the room at the supportive group of friends from over the years. "This is about Katherine and her baby."

We were all dabbing our eyes and shaking our heads in mutual agreement.

"Jett would know if he were the father," Olivia prompted.

I looked at Leslie for an affirmation. "I don't know," She sighed. "I was so upset with Katherine, we didn't speak for years. She never told me if Jett was the father."

"Do you think he might still be in town?" Sarah asked.

"Maybe he is. Let's call Detective Lincoln and see if he

has a cell phone number or hotel since he questioned Jett earlier," I said with determination. "He may be able to clear up this quickly."

We all gathered our bags and coats and made our way to the lobby. The car was waiting to take us to the Dallas police station.

"Does anyone else feel like a couple of White Castle hamburgers or maybe a Jack-in-the-Box?" Olivia sheepishly asked as we piled into the roomy car.

"You are the only one I know who could eat at a time like this, Olivia Rivers!" Cassandra rebuked her.

"Protein keeps the brain in tip top performance and that's what we need right now," she protested.

"I think you're right," Shane agreed. "We should get something to eat before we talk with Jett. This might be a long day."

Shane's words could not have rung more true. This would be a long day … and a day we would look back on and shudder!

SIXTEEN

After a quick lunch on the go, we arrived at the police station. Shane had called Detective Lincoln on the way and shared with him the new revelation about Katherine. He was waiting in the lobby when we arrived and ushered us into a large conference room.

"Shane, ladies, take a seat. Olivia," he addressed her as he gingerly pulled out a chair and gestured for her to sit. Olivia thanked him and sat down, allowing Lincoln to help her scoot her chair towards the table. She looked up at the tall detective and smiled coyly.

Cassandra didn't miss the exchange and began tittering in her chair. She attempted to hide her laughter, but Olivia was not amused by her antics and glared at her to stop.

"This makes finding Monica Gold that much more significant," the detective said as he crossed his arms and looked at the wipe-off board covered with diagrams and photos of the crime scene. "Is Jett Rollins the father?" he pointedly asked me.

"I would have no way of knowing since I didn't speak to Jett or Katherine after I left for London," I reminded him. "Leslie was never told who the father was or if she had the baby. Katherine moved back west to stay with an aunt and was soon hired by the soap," I concluded.

"Seems like Mr. Rollins should be able to clear this up," Lincoln said and sat on the edge of the table closest to Olivia, his arms still crossed in an authoritative manner. "I was able to reach him on his cell phone and he's on his way now," he told us.

There was a knock on the door and an officer opened it abruptly as he escorted Jett into the room. All eyes were on him as he shook Lincoln's hand and took an empty chair next to Sarah.

"Jett, I'm Shane Spencer," Shane offered his hand.

"Nice to meet you," he said and shook hands across the table. "Amelia," he greeted me as he sat back down, a strained expression on his face.

"Jett, I need to ask you some questions about your relationship with Katherine Gold," Lincoln said as he stood up and began pacing the crowded room. "Were you aware that Katherine found out she was pregnant after graduation?"

A hush fell across the room as all eyes were focused on Jett and his reaction to the news. I tried not to look at him. His face registered total surprise and it took him a few minutes to collect his thoughts.

"Preganant? Katherine? No, I was not aware of that," Jett whispered and paused.

Lincoln cleared his throat and continued, "Could it be possible you were the father?"

Jett's fists clenched and he looked down at the table. "I highly doubt it," he responded.

"Were you not intimately involved with Miss Gold around the time of graduation?" Lincoln persisted. He began pacing behind Jett's chair.

"Yes, I'm not denying that we were intimate. It was just

the one time," he stated uncomfortably and glanced in my direction. Shane held my hand under the table for support and gave it a gentle squeeze.

"It only takes one time, my mother taught me," Olivia said sardonically to Jett. "And it only takes one time to be a cheater," she said as she leaned across the table towards Jett.

"Olivia, try to control yourself," Cassandra hissed under her breath.

"If he had kept his pants zipped, we wouldn't be having this conversation," she snapped back.

"Katherine never told me about a pregnancy but I am one hundred percent sure I could not be the father!" Jett declared.

"How can you be that certain?" Lincoln questioned the humiliated man.

"My wife and I just went through infertility studies. When I said the twins were a miracle for us, it wasn't an exaggeration," he said uneasily and swallowed hard. "I found out I was sterile. We had to use a sperm donor to conceive the twins," Jett revealed.

"Wow, this is better than *Jerry Springer!* Sterile!" Olivia said dramatically.

"Show some compassion, Liv!" Sarah implored her friend and slapped her hand for emphasis.

"Tough break, Jett," Olivia said sincerely and tried to compose herself.

"Any idea who the father might be since Mr. Rollins is ruled out?" Lincoln asked us.

"Leslie? Do you have any ideas about who else she was seeing?" I asked.

"She dated a lot of men and we weren't on speaking

terms after the whole Jett incident," she reiterated.

"I'm pretty sure I know who Katherine was seeing... Carson Craig."

I remembered Carson Craig as the man about campus, the all-star football player and one of the most popular guys at SMU. I had never heard Katherine mention him, but it wouldn't surprise me if they had hooked up at one time since they would almost be like a "Barbie and Ken" super couple with her golden hair and his muscular build.

"Did Carson attend the reunion?" the detective asked Jett.

"Yes, he was at the cocktail party and the game. We were fraternity brothers and a group of us had block seats at homecoming. He lives here in Dallas. It shouldn't be hard to look him up," Jett suggested.

"I'll have a car go by and pick him up. Stay put, OK?" he instructed as the door shut firmly behind him.

There was an awkward silence in the room. No one knew quite what to say. For once, I was glad Olivia didn't have a smart comment.

Sarah was the first to speak. "Did you bring any pictures of the twins with you?" She gently asked Jett breaking the ice.

"Yes, I have a few with me," he said and removed his wallet from the back pocket of his jeans. "This is Bonnie and the little guy on the left is Jacob," he showed her. He seemed to be glad to have something to focus his attention on other than the interrogation.

"How beautiful, Jett. You're lucky," she smiled sweetly at him and handed back the photos. "And your wife? How long have you been married?"

"About ten years now. Laura's at home with the twins. I really miss them," he said as he placed his wallet back in his pocket. "Laura and the kids are everything to me," he said.

I gave Shane's hand another squeeze. Everything had turned out for the best. I had my beautiful Emma and handsome Charlie. I missed them so much right now. And I was blessed to have found such a wonderful man—the person with whom I was supposed to be with. I knew that with one hundred percent certainty.

The door swung abruptly open and Lincoln strode into the room. Everyone jumped involuntarily at his quick entrance.

"Carson Craig is missing," Lincoln announced. "His wife Shelly said he never came home after the game Saturday. She says his phone keeps going directly to voicemail."

"I was with Carson in the parking lot," Jett said shaking his head in confusion. "He was getting his car keys out and we were saying our goodbyes. He seemed fine."

"Where were you parked?" Lincoln quickly asked.

"The campus parking garage, third level," Jett recalled.

Lincoln left the room at a jog and the door slammed once again. This was becoming more and more bizarre. First Monica was missing. Now Carson?

"I should have never left Monica alone," Sarah said as tears began forming in the corners of her eyes. "Something bad has happened. If I had only been there with her," she admonished herself.

"Then you might be missing too," Olivia reminded her. "Think about it, Sarah! Someone killed Katherine. The probable father of Katherine's baby is missing along with her sister. Someone could have hurt you if you were in the way."

"Do you think Monica is responsible for Carson's disappearance?" Shane asked me quietly.

"No way, Monica was always the sweetest girl," I quickly responded.

Lincoln walked back in with a grave look on his face. "I ran Mr. Craig's license plates. His car is still in the SMU parking garage," he said approaching Jett. "Did you see anyone or anything suspicious while you were saying goodbye to him?"

Jett paused and began rubbing his chin. "No. Just the usual gang from the old days, nothing out of the ordinary," he remarked.

"The gang from the old days? Who would that have been?"

"Let's see. There was Ethan Talent, Frank Dupree, Rachel Collins, Holly Smith, Alex Whittaker…"

"Wait, Jett, back up. Did you say Holly Smith?" I stopped him abruptly.

"Yes, Holly. Why?"

"Holly had a huge crush on Carson, remember?" I turned towards Leslie for confirmation. "She was almost obsessive about it. She wore his campaign pins all over her backpack when he was nominated for homecoming king, remember?"

"Yes, she was head over heels in love with him," Leslie agreed. She drove everyone crazy running around campus screaming in her bull horn to vote for Carson. I thought she mind end up actually costing him some votes. She was almost rabid."

"Just like she is rabid about Gamma Phi Beta?" Cassandra pointed out. "She was very pushy Saturday about donations and bequeathing in wills."

"I did call her the 'Grim Reaper.' Maybe she's worse than

we thought. Maybe she's not so harmless after all," Olivia spoke truthfully.

"Did you see Holly Smith with Carson Craig?" Detective Lincoln asked Jett.

"Yeah," Jett answered with a faraway look in his eye. "When we were all going our separate ways, she was pulling on his arm and saying something about Carson needing to walk her to her car. I didn't think anything of it. It's Holly. She's always been a bit of a pain in the neck."

"Where's Holly Smith live?" Lincoln inquired of our group.

"She lives in Monterey, California. She's some kind of marine biologist, I remember reading in our sorority newsletter," Leslie added.

"Marine biologist? Leslie, marine biologists have access to marine animals like the blue ringed octopus!" I shouted and grabbed her arm. "I think we know who killed Katherine!"

"I knew she was creepy, but wow, she really is scary," Olivia remarked.

"We've got to find Holly and fast," Lincoln shouted and flung the door open. "Rodriguez, put out an APB for Holly Smith of Monterey, California, STAT!" he commanded. Everyone began scurrying around the squad room.

"Oh my goodness, Amelia! Do you really think Holly is capable of killing Katherine?" Sarah asked obviously stunned by the revelation of the new information. "She seemed to be so happy the newspaper had Katherine on the front page Saturday."

"Yes, she did seem proud. Not jealous in the least," Cassandra added.

"Proud our sorority was getting notoriety that our most famous member was on the front page of *The Dallas Morning News*. It's always been Gamma Phi first with Holly," I said as I began to realize what was unfolding in front of us.

"Holly took the presidency to heart. She's still very active in the alumnae association," Leslie added.

"What would cause her to kill Katherine?" Shane asked puzzled. "This doesn't make sense to me."

"I think with Katherine dead, her celebrity status would be even more elevated like Marilyn Monroe or Anna Nicole Smith," I surmised.

"And Gamma Phi would have an 'infamous' celebrity member," Sarah said. "I think we get it."

"And," Cassandra added rising to her feet, "if she were really obsessed with Carson, she could get Katherine out of the way and have him all to herself."

"Leslie, do you think Holly found out about Carson and Katherine?" I asked as I turned towards my talented former roommate.

"I remember something did happen around graduation at the sorority house."

"What? Tell us Leslie!" Sarah encouraged her to continue.

"I left our apartment after the 'incident' with Katherine and Jett. Sorry, Jett, but hey, it happened. I stayed at the Gamma Phi house for the next week while I packed up my things in the apartment whenever Katherine wasn't around. I couldn't stand to stay there with her after what she did. I remember during my time at the sorority house Holly was acting very strange," she established.

"How could you tell, Leslie?" Olivia interjected. "She

seems to be certifiable most of the time. By the way, anyone have some peanuts or crackers or something to munch on? I'm starving!"

Cassandra shot a nasty look in Olivia's direction. "I'm sorry, Leslie, continue!"

"I would describe it as a full blown melt-down. We were all hanging out in the living room watching *Falcon Crest* when I remember one of the pledges running downstairs saying Holly had locked herself in one of the bathroom stalls and was hysterical."

"What happened?" Sarah asked breathlessly.

"We went upstairs and she was sobbing uncontrollably. She was ripping up pictures and flushing them down the toilet. I didn't see the pictures, but she was definitely upset," Leslie concluded.

Poor Holly. She had been a victim of Katherine as well. I imagine she found out about the relationship with Carson and lost it. I was assuming a lot, but the pieces fit together in a twisted love triangle.

"We had to get the house mother to come up and talk to her. I thought we might have to call for help. She carried on for hours and we were all very concerned," Leslie remembered.

"Did she ever say what happened?" I asked guessing she was heartbroken.

"All she said was that she had been a fool to believe him. She never said who he was but one minute she was crying, the next minute she was throwing things. She was like Dr. Jekyll and Mr. Hyde. It was rather frightening. We were all up most of the night feeling apprehensive. We all thought she was nuts," Leslie confirmed.

"How bizarre! I never heard about this," I spoke up.

"It fits the time frame when Katherine and Carson were dating. They decided to call it quits a few days before graduation. Carson was drunk at the frat house and said he was leaving for graduate school and didn't need to be tied down to anyone," Jett remembered.

"Do you think he knew Katherine was pregnant?" I asked Jett.

"Carson's a standup guy. I can't imagine he would turn his back on Katherine if he knew. The way I understood it, she was leaving to audition in LA and he had plans to go grad school at Chapel Hill," he said.

Detective Lincoln interrupted suddenly, "We just got a break. We were able to track the GPS on Monica Gold's phone to Harry Hines Boulevard. We're heading over there now." He slapped the doorframe in his excitement.

"I don't want to sit here and wait. We need to follow them," Sarah said and flung her thrift shop handbag over her arm. "Monica needs us!"

"I'll make sure the driver keeps up. Come on!" Cassandra shouted and we all pushed our chairs away from the conference room table.

We could not have anticipated the danger that awaited Monica and Carson as we followed the speeding SWAT team that moved stealthily towards Monica's GPS signal.

SEVENTEEN

*D*etective Lincoln was garbed in his bullet proof vest with bold yellow letters spelling POLICE across the front. We waited behind the police barricade as the SWAT team took their places around an abandoned building on Harry Hines. The area was run down and the parking lot dimly lit with overgrown weeds, broken glass and debris scattered everywhere.

The captain of the team came over and updated Lincoln. "We were able to thread a tactical camera through the roof and have established audio and visual feed on the female suspect. She is armed and holding two hostages at gunpoint," he said in a rapid staccato.

"Good job Jacobs," Lincoln said and patted him on the back. "I want you to put Mrs. Spencer and Miss Lane in the command center. I think they might be able to help negotiate with our suspect," he instructed. He put on a headset and began barking orders. "Let me know when everyone is in their positions," we could hear him instructing.

"Follow me ladies," Captain Jacobs commanded.

We left Olivia, Cassandra, Shane and Sarah huddled safely behind the barricade. As we entered the mobile headquarter, I noticed the small interior was filled with computers, flat screen monitors and a variety of machinery. Two officers were seated, studying the video feed and continually updating the team.

"Put these on," Jacobs told us. We were immediately able to hear the conversation between the officers as well as the audio feed from inside the building in our headsets. Leslie and I both stared at the monitors and were afraid to speak.

I could hear Lincoln's voice. "Holly Smith, this is Detective Lincoln with the Dallas Metropolitan Police. We have the building surrounded. Release your hostages and come out with your hands up," he shouted.

"Never! I will never surrender. You will have to kill me before I give up!" Holly screamed in return.

"We are requesting the release of Miss Gold and Mr. Craig unharmed. Please send them out immediately," the detective requested.

"No. She ruined my life. Don't you understand? She took Carson from me!" Holly screeched from the inside of the dark building.

"Let's talk about this Holly," Lincoln calmly suggested, trying to bring her anger under control.

"I'm not falling for your games. What I want you can't give me. I want the life I was supposed to have. I want the life I was supposed to have with Carson. He was mine and she took him away from me!" she shrieked.

"She's not cooperating, Jacobs," Lincoln said into his headset. "What's the status?"

"We've got a clear shot, Lincoln. Just say the word," the captain could be heard replying.

"We want to prevent casualties. Let's try to talk her out if possible. Let's get Mrs. Spencer and Miss Lane in contact with her."

"We need to keep her calm," Jacobs instructed me. "We are going to call Miss Gold's cell phone and hope she picks up. Try to talk her into letting the hostages go," he said in a reassuring tone.

I nodded in quiet affirmation as Monica's cell phone could be heard ringing over the audio fee. In the monitor, we could see Holly motion with her gun for Monica to hand her the cell phone.

"Holly, it's Amelia," I said as my voice trembled slightly. "Holly, you don't want to hurt anyone. Please let Monica and Carson go," I implored her.

"I'm not letting them go. She was in on it," Holly yelled into the phone. "She covered up for her sister all these years. She helped that whore take him away from me!" she continued to rant.

"Holly, no one could ever love Carson like you do," I tried to assuage her. "Katherine didn't mean anything to him. She did the same thing to me with Jett. I know how you feel, Holly, but think about what you are doing," I begged to no avail.

"I know exactly what I'm doing. I'm making them pay for ruining my life," she shouted. "What do I have? I have NOTHING and NO ONE to love me. She took the one man I truly ever loved and he made a fool of me."

"She seems to be more agitated," Leslie noted. "Try talking to her about the sorority," she suggested.

"Holly, I implore you to think about the sorority. You will ruin Gamma Phi's reputation if you hurt them," I attempted to reason with her.

"I don't care anymore. It's too late. Screw it all!" she yelled and hung up.

"Captain, I'm in position to take the shot," an officer could be heard.

We could hear Holly demanding answers from Carson over the tactical feed. "Tell me! Tell me you loved me more than her. Tell me you made a horrible mistake! How could you love that whore?"

"Holly, Holly, calm down," Carson pleaded with her. "I never knew how you felt about me. Let's talk about this, please!"

"You didn't know? You didn't know how I felt about you? How could you say that? I was totally devoted to you. How can you say you didn't know? Was I that invisible?" she shouted at the top of her voice.

"Amelia, she is crazy! She sounds like she did that night at the sorority house," Leslie said shaken up.

"On my mark," Captain Jacobs ordered.

"You men are all alike. You just want a quick jump in the sack. That's all I ever was to you!" Holly accused Carson.

"Holly, we were two drunken kids. It didn't mean anything," Carson acknowledged.

"It meant something to me. It meant a whole lot to me!" She was livid now and her voice sounded like it was filled with so much hate. "She couldn't be happy with every other man on campus. She had to take you away from me too!"

"Holly, there never was a you and me. We were drunk!" Carson reasoned.

"I was not drunk! I love you Carson Craig and I loved you then. Don't you get it? No one could ever love you like I do. No one!" she sobbed and waved the gun around in his face.

"Put the gun down, Holly," Monica yelled. "Put the gun down before someone else gets hurt."

"SHUT UP! SHUT UP MONICA! Don't tell me what to do!"

"Take the shot," Jacobs ordered.

I turned away from the monitor when I heard gunfire. I glanced back to see the SWAT team kick the door down and flood the building with smoke. I held my breath praying Monica and Carson were not injured. I watched as the EMS workers rushed through the front entrance with a gurney. I took off my headset and grabbed Leslie's hand as we rushed out the door towards our friends huddled behind the police barricade.

"I hope Monica and Carson are fine," Sarah said in an unsteady voice. "I will never forgive myself if something happened to her."

"Sarah, sweetheart, let's just pray everyone makes it out alive," Cassandra said and gave her a supportive hug. Sarah buried her head in Cassandra's shoulder and began to cry.

I stood stunned. I couldn't believe what had transpired tonight and couldn't believe Holly had been behind such a heinous murder! How well do we truly know those around us?

Detective Lincoln walked next to a weeping Monica Gold. We all rushed forward to help her.

"Monica, are you all right?" Leslie asked as she wiped a smudge of dirt off her tear stained face. "I can't believe this happened!"

"I can't believe it either. One minute she was talking with me about Katherine and a memorial service on campus and the next minute she snapped and shoved a gun in my face! This has been a nightmare!"

"It was a mistake to leave you alone," Sarah told her. "We had no idea it was Holly!"

Just then a rather beat up and tired Carson Craig was wheeled out on a gurney. He had a cut lip, black eye and what appeared to be several contusions on his head. He had definitely received the brunt of Holly's anger.

"Brother, it's good to see you," Jett exclaimed.

"I didn't think I was going to make it out of there alive," Carson said relieved.

"What happened, Carson?" Jett asked.

"She just snapped. She asked me to walk her to her car and when we got over to the mini-van, she slid open the back door and that's all I remember. I think she knocked me out. I've got a pretty big bump on the back of my head. I don't remember anything except waking up here tied in a chair. I have no idea what set her off!" Carson said earnestly.

"I do Carson," Monica stated as she walked over the gurney. "I told her I thought Katherine's son should be at his mother's memorial service."

"Katherine has a son?" Carson asked incredulously. "I didn't know that."

"Yes and he looks a lot like his father," Monica said and rubbed his arm. "He's nineteen years old and a sophomore at SMU. Katherine was moving back to Dallas to be closer to him," she revealed.

As Monica's news sunk in, Carson began to look around at the faces surrounding him. "Are you telling me that Katherine had a baby and it was MY baby?" he speculated.

"Yes, Carson. She knew you were on your way to graduate school and she thought it would be best not to ruin your plans," Monica told him as tears rolled down her face. "I didn't agree with her decision not to tell you, but she felt it was the best thing to do at the time."

"I have a son? I have a son!" Carson was starting to break down. "Katherine and I have a son," he wept. Monica leaned over and kissed him, the realization that Katherine was gone, the understanding of the lost years of watching his son grow up and the comprehension that this hellish nightmare was over must have been too much to bear for him. We were all crying now. We were thankful Monica and Carson were going to be OK.

Detective Lincoln walked over and shook hands with Carson and Monica. He then came over to me and shook my hand. "Mrs. Spencer, I owe you a huge debt. Had it not been for your persistence in this case, we might not have discovered the link to the missing tiara."

I smiled at the handsome officer and gave him a friendly smile. "I think we're even. You saved my friends' lives. I will always be grateful for that," I told him.

"This is an unexpected love fest," Olivia said as she approached the two of us.

"And may I say it was an unexpected pleasure meeting you, Miss Rivers," Lincoln said as he gently shook Olivia's hand as their eyes locked, the electricity between the two almost visible. "If you are planning on extending your stay, I would be honored if you'd allow me to take you to this great spot I know in Fort Worth for some line dancing," he offered.

"Line dancing? You, the dashing Detective Lincoln, line dances? This is just too good to be true!" Olivia laughed and threw back her head. "Here's my cell phone number. Why don't you call me tomorrow and we can take it from there?" she suggested and winked at him.

"Ladies, Shane, Jett, it's been a pleasure. Duty calls. I'm

back to work," Lincoln said and walked back towards the crime scene, a big smile visible on his rugged face.

The EMS workers carefully shut the ambulance door. Carson Craig was on his way to Medical City Dallas, Monica Gold riding by his side. We were on our way back to our hotel, tired and weary, but grateful things had turned out as well as they did.

EIGHTEEN

A few weeks later, we flew back to Dallas for a memorial service for Katherine organized by the producers of *The Rich and the Lost*. It was a private affair for friends and family held at Perkins Chapel on campus. A large tasteful portrait of Katherine was framed and placed on an easel at the front of the church. Large urns filled with her favorite yellow roses flanked her picture.

Shane, Cassandra, Sarah, Olivia and I sat with Monica and her nephew Craig. He did look much like Carson, but had his mother's smoldering eyes. Carson and his wife Shelly sat on the other side of Craig. Leslie could not join us since she was in the midst of filming a movie with Ron Howard.

The service was a very respectful tribute to Katherine and both Monica and Craig spoke about what a wonderful sister and mother she had been. There was not a dry eye in the church as she shared with everyone her stories of visiting Katherine during college weekends and what a wonderful job she had done raising Craig as a single mom.

Craig spoke about the unconditional love his mother had given him, privately sheltering him from the paparazzi and the spotlight. She had sent him to good schools, traveled extensively with him, encouraged him to attend her alma-mater, and to follow in his father's footsteps. She had explained to him that one day he would know his father, that the timing had been wrong, but to know he was very much loved.

Craig had an opportunity to spend time with Carson and Shelly at their home and had slowly been introduced to their children, Sam and Ryan. They were thrilled to have a big brother who played football at SMU. Now they had someone to cheer on at the games. Carson and Craig were still getting to know each other, but so far, it had gone smoothly. He was a great kid and Carson was very proud of him.

"Katherine did a great job raising Craig," Carson told us at the reception in Dallas Hall. "I just wish she could be here today to see us together," he said and proudly looked over at Craig Gold.

"I think she's smiling down on both of you. She would be very pleased to know how you and Shelly have welcomed him into your family," I told him.

"I'm glad to know Katherine had a side to her that was soft and maternal," Carson said.

It seemed so strange to me after all this time, I was finally able to look back on my college years with a certain sentimental feeling. I no longer looked back and felt as if everything that happened was a nightmare. We had all come out of it a bit scratched and bruised, but better people for having known her.

Olivia walked over, hand in hand with Detective Lincoln. The two had been flying back and forth between Dogwood Cove and Dallas ever since their night of line dancing. It was good to see Liv with someone who could not only stand up to her, but hold her interest as well. She deserved someone like Matt Lincoln.

"What are you smiling about, Amelia?" she asked.

I sighed and answered, "I was just thinking about coming full circle. I can't believe Katherine brought us all together. For that, I am thankful."

"You seem distant, Amelia. What's up?" Cassandra asked as she crossed the marble floors of the rotunda of Dallas Hall. She looked the part of a best dressed diva in a gold Armani suit in Katherine's honor.

"So much has happened since we left Dogwood Cove for the reunion. My head is still spinning," I admitted to her.

Cassandra nodded. "Yes, I imagine you are tired from packing up the tea room."

"Not really, I didn't have much packing since Sarah bought it lock, stock and barrel," I told her and smiled. I waved at Sarah who had brought Jake White with her for the trip. It seemed owning the tea room wasn't the only thing new in Sarah's life.

"I found a new friend," Olivia said and looked up at her handsome detective.

"Friends are we now? That's not what you said last night," he teased her.

"Matt Lincoln, you hush before I hog tie you!" she threatened and smacked his arm in warning.

"Watch her, Lincoln. She means it," Cassandra advised him.

"Hopefully she won't have a good reason to hog tie me. I intend to keep you very happy," he said speaking to no one but Olivia.

"And how about you, Amelia?" Olivia inquired. "Are you going to take it easy for a while?"

"I think I will enjoy working with Shane on our new tea blends. I've got some great ideas for Smoky Mountain Coffee, Herb and Tea Company," I responded.

"Yes, yes she does," Shane said joining our little group. "I'm looking forward to having Amelia home for a while."

"What about our tea infused chocolate truffles? We've got to get started on those," Cassandra reminded me.

"We do indeed," I cheerfully agreed.

"Chocolate and tea. I love the idea," Shane stated.

"So do our chefs at Reynolds's in Paris. They want to meet with Amelia right away," she told him.

"How soon?" he asked.

"Shane, if I didn't know better, I would think you were trying to get rid of me," I accused him.

"Never, I think you need a change of scenery after all you've been through. Paris and recipe development would be just what the doctor ordered," Shane told me.

"What do you say, Amelia?" Cassandra raised her eyebrows. "Next week?"

"Next week? Are you serious?" I couldn't believe she was suggesting I pack for a trip so soon.

"Next week will be fine, Cassandra. Now that we don't have the tea room, we don't have to worry about the day to day running of things. It gives us time for new pursuits," Shane shared. "Amelia will be happy to join you in Paris."

"What about Emma and Charlie?" I reminded him.

"We'll manage. Christmas break is coming up shortly. Maybe we could join you in Paris for the holidays?" he suggested.

Christmas in Paris? I couldn't imagine not being home for the holidays, but he was right. I wouldn't have the busy holiday schedule with the tea room for private parties, all the extra cooking and decorating. I had been looking forward to a relaxing time at home with my family this year.

"I better finish my Christmas shopping then," I said joyfully and clapped my hands as I began the mental checklist of what I would have to do to get ready.

"What's all the excitement about?" Sarah asked as she and Jake walked up to the group. She looked very un-costume-like today wearing a simple black jacket and matching pants. No hat, no big jewelry, no funky hairdo. I think Sarah was finding she could express her creativity through her culinary presentations at the tea room. She was finally stretching her wings.Running her own business seemed to satisfy her.

"Amelia is going to Paris with Cassandra for Christmas," Olivia told her.

"Paris? Oh, how romantic! I've always wanted to go to Paris," Sarah sighed.

"Why don't you then?" Cassandra insisted. "Why don't we all go to Paris?"

"Have you lost your mind? It's almost Christmas!" Olivia informed her.

"So take a break. Sarah, is the tea room going to be open the entire holiday season?" Cassandra asked.

"We will be closed December twenty-fourth through New Year's Day," Sarah said thoughtfully.

Cassandra turned toward Olivia. "What are your holiday plans?" she pried.

"I don't know. I've got to take care of the ranch. I wasn't planning anything special," she answered.

"Can you get the ranch hands to help? Why don't you and Lincoln plan on joining us for Christmas and New

Year's in Paris? I think it would be wonderful!" Cassandra was excited about our new plans.

"Works for me," Sarah agreed. "I'm sure it will be hard for me to get away for a while, but I'll manage it," she said confidently.

"I'm definitely in!" I told the group.

"Liv? We're waiting on you," Cassandra pressured. "Oh come on! Those animals will be fine without you for a while. What do you say?"

"I say, 'To the Traveling Tea Ladies' and to Paris!" Olivia squealed and gave each of us a hug.

"You'll get used to it," Shane told Lincoln as he shook his head in amusement.

"They are definitely not a boring group," Matt Lincoln said as he smiled and put his arms around his little red haired spit fire. "Definitely not boring!"

~THE END~

How to Make
the Perfect Pot of Tea

In the same amount of time that you measure level scoops of coffee for the coffee maker and add ounces of water, you can prepare a cup or pot of tea.

Step 1: Select your tea pot.

Porcelain or pottery is the better choice versus silver plated tea pots which can impart a slightly metallic taste. Make sure your tea pot is clean with no soapy residue and prime your tea pot by filling it with hot water, letting it sit for a few minutes and then pouring the water out so that your pot will stay warm longer!

Step 2: WATER, WATER, WATER!

Begin with the cleanest, filtered, de-chlorinated water you can. Good water makes a huge difference. Many of my tea room guests have asked why their tea doesn't taste the same at home. The chlorine in the water is often the culprit of sabotaging a great pot of tea.

Be sure your water comes to a rolling boil and quickly remove it. If you let it boil continuously, you will boil out all the oxygen and be left with a "flat" tasting tea. Please do not microwave your water. It can cause your water to "super boil" and lead to third degree burns. If you are in a situation where you don't have a full kitchen, purchase an electric tea kettle to quickly and easily make your hot water.

And NEVER, NEVER, EVER MAKE TEA IN A COFFEE MAKER! I cannot tell you how I cringe when asked if it's okay. Coffee drinkers don't want to taste tea and tea drinkers don't want to taste coffee. Period! End of story! Golden rule—no coffee makers!

Now that we've cleared that up, let's measure out our tea!

Step 3: Measure Out Your Tea.

It's easy! The formula is one teaspoon of loose tea per 8 ounces of water. For example, if you are using a 4 cup teapot, you would use 4 teaspoons of tea, maybe a little less depending on your personal taste. Measure your tea and place inside a "t-sac" or paper filter made for tea, infuser ball, or tea filter basket. Place the tea inside your pot and now you're ready for steeping.

Step 4: Steeping Times and Temperature.

This is the key!

Black teas—Steep for 3-4minutes with boiling water (212 degrees)

Herbals, Tisanes and Rooibos—boiling water, Steep for 7 minutes.

Oolongs—195 degree Water. Steep for 3 minutes.

Whites and Greens—Steaming water—175 degrees. Steep for 3 minutes.

Essie's Key Lime Pie

"Sarah, calm down!" Olivia scolded. "Amelia should be the one that's crying! You know she puts her heart and soul into everything she makes there. I know I am going to miss your Grandmother's Key Lime pie!" —Chapter One

One 8 ounce block of cream cheese, softened at room temperature
2 cans of sweetened condensed milk
½ cup key lime juice (fresh or bottled, NOT LIME JUICE!)
1 graham cracker pie crust

Place block of cream cheese in a large bowl. Using an electric mixture, whip cream cheese until smooth. Combine sweetened condensed milk and cream cheese on high speed until mixture is ultra smooth with no lumps. Add key lime juice and blend thoroughly. Pour into graham cracker crust and refrigerate for six to eight hours before serving. Garnish with a dollop of almond cream or fresh whipped cream and top with a mint leaf or slivered strawberry!

Note from Melanie: My grandmother, Essie, always made this pie when we came for a visit. She had a key lime tree in her backyard and would make this with freshly squeezed juice. Remember, REAL key limes are yellow and your pie should be a pale yellow, never fake green!

Southern Peach Iced Tea

"I also had a key lime pie in a cooler in back of lady bug along with a gallon of my secret recipe peach iced tea. That surprise would be for later." Amelia Spencer —Chapter One

One cup sweet tea concentrate
Three 11.3 ounce cans peach nectar
¼ cup fresh squeezed lemon juice
Water

Pour peach nectar into a one gallon container or pitcher. Add ¼ cup lemon juice and one cup of sweet tea concentrate. Add water to top of container and stir until well mixed. Serve over ice!

Note from Melanie: This is my "Secret Recipe" and worth at least a million dollars! We had guests take gallons of this home, so beware if you make it once, you will always be asked to make it for every family get-together, Bunco night, PTA meeting. You get the picture!

Cassandra's Lynchburg Lemonade

"Wait a minute, wait a minute," Cassandra called out, her hands full of a pitcher of something icy. "I've brought the party; my own version of Lynchburg Lemonade."

—Chapter One

1 cup Jack Daniels whiskey

1 cup Triple Sec

1 cup sweet and sour mix

4 cups lemon-lime soda

Combine all four ingredients and serve over ice. Garnish with long stemmed cherry.

A Note from Melanie: Lynchburg, Tennessee is worth a visit, even if you are not a fan of Jack Daniels. You can take a tour of the famous facility that put Lynchburg on the map!

Sarah's Fried Green Tomatoes

"Hey, Sarah," I jumped up and helped her with a rather large tray loaded down with all kinds of covered casserole dishes. "What have you got in here?"

"Oh, just my corn fritters, fried green tomatoes and potato salad," she announced, rather proud of herself!

—Chapter One

    4 large green tomatoes

    1 ½ cups buttermilk

    1 tablespoon salt

    1 teaspoon pepper

    1 cup all purpose flour

    1 cup cornmeal (self rising preferable)

    3 cups vegetable oil

Cut tomatoes in ¼ inch slices. Place tomatoes in shallow dish and pour buttermilk over tomatoes. Sprinkle with salt and pepper. Combine flour and cornmeal in a shallow dish. Remove tomato slices from buttermilk and dredge each side of each slice in the cornmeal mixture. Heat vegetable oil in cast iron skillet on medium heat. Fry tomato slices in small batches until golden brown. Drain on paper towels and sprinkle with additional salt if desired. Best served hot.

Note from Melanie: Nothing is more southern than fried green tomatoes! Our area is famous for Grainger County tomatoes and we look forward to this seasonal delicacy each summer.

Tennessee Corn Fritters

She smiled at me and gave me a quick hug as I set down her assortment of covered casseroles and snuck a corn fritter while they were still warm. Amelia Spencer —Chapter One

3 cups vegetable oil for frying

1 cup of all-purpose flour—sifted

1 teaspoon baking powder

½ teaspoon salt

¼ teaspoon granulated sugar

1 beaten egg

½ cup milk

1 tablespoon vegetable shortening, melted

1 can of corn kernels, drained or fresh off the cob

(about 4 ears of corn)

Heat oil in deep pan or small counter-top fryer to 365 degrees. Careful, oil is hot and will spatter! In a bowl, combine flour, baking powder, salt and sugar. In a separate bowl, combine beaten egg, milk and melted shortening. Stir flour mixture into egg mixture until thoroughly mixed. Add corn. Drop batter by spoonful, CAREFULLY in the hot oil and fry until golden brown. Drain fritters on paper towel and serve warm. Makes 12 corn fritters.

Note From Melanie: Caution! These are addictive. You can sprinkle with powdered sugar and they become more of a sweet. I can remember my first corn fritter at The Kapok Tree Inn in Clear Water, Florida. I thought I had died and gone to heaven!

Chocolate Chip Scones

I quickly washed my hands, slipped on my black and white toile apron and began preparations to make a quadruple batch of chocolate chip scones at the birthday girl's request. Sure, there are plenty of scone mixes out there that many other tea rooms used, but nothing was as good as making them from scratch. Yes, it was time consuming, but worth it! Amelia Spencer—Chapter Two

2 cups all purpose flour

1/3 cup sugar

2 teaspoons baking powder

1 stick butter, chilled

½ cup semi-sweet chocolate chips

2 eggs

2 Tablespoons vanilla extract

Heavy whipping cream or buttermilk—approximately ¼ to ½ cup (You will eyeball and add as needed)

Cane sugar for topping

In a large bowl, combine flour, sugar, and baking powder. Cut butter into thin slices. Using pastry blender, cut butter into flour mixture until it resembles coarse meal. Add chocolate chips and mix. In a separate bowl, combine eggs and vanilla. Add to flour mixture and pour cream in a little at a time until mixture is sticky and dough forms. Just eyeball it and add just enough to moisten the dough. On a well floured surface, gently roll out dough to a ½ inch thickness. Flour a round biscuit cutter. Gently push straight down into dough and lift straight up. Do not twist cutter as that will break the air bubbles in the dough and you will not get a scones that is high. Place on baking sheet covered in parchment paper or silicone baking sheet. Sprinkle with cane sugar for a sweet and crunchy topping. Bake at 400 degrees for 23-25 minutes until slightly brown on top.

Note from Melanie: I recommend freezing for two or more hours to increase a nice rise and split of scones. Serve with almond cream, lemon curd or strawberry preserves. Before all my British readers contact me to tell me these are "not traditional" because of the chocolate chips, I dare you to try them! They are so moist, clotted cream and toppings are unnecessary!

Amelia's Famous Almond Cream

I took the pie out of the cooler and sliced four healthy pieces. A little dollop of my famous almond cream and a sliver of strawberry on top; that should do it! I placed the pie and steaming mugs of coffee on one of Olivia's trays and joined the girls on the patio. Amelia Spencer—Chapter One

One pint heavy whipping cream

¼ cup confectioner's sugar

3 teaspoons almond or imitation almond extract

Place above ingredients in large bowl. Using an electric mixer on low to medium speed, whip all ingredients together until cream begins to thicken. Increase mixer speed to high and whip until soft peaks form. You can keep this refrigerated for up to one week. Simply rewhip before serving. It's perfect on scones, cake, pie, trifles and desserts. Good enough to eat alone!

Note from Melanie: I came up with this recipe on the fly when I was out of sour cream and vanilla extract needed to make "Mock Devonshire Cream." I looked in the pantry, and all I had was almond extract. It was such a hit, it was requested by our guests to take home. I would be strung up by my toe nails if I didn't have almond cream available!

Olivia's Lemonade Iced Tea

"Oh, the lemonade iced tea sounds perfect! Thank you!" And it was! Cold, slightly sweet and tart at the same time. Amelia Spencer—Chapter Four

3 quarts fresh water

2 Large Luzianne Family sized tea bags —Yes, Luzianne! They are a blend of 3 black teas perfect for iced tea!

¾ cup of sugar or more depending on your personal taste

One 12 ounce can frozen lemonade concentrate. I prefer Minute Maid.

Bring water to a boil. Place tea bags in the bottom of a gallon container or pitcher with tea tag draped over the side and secured. Pour boiling water over tea bags, just enough to cover. Place lid over container and allow to steep for EXACTLY 5 MINUTES! Remove bags and discard. Add thawed lemonade concentrate, sugar and cold water while stirring to dissolve lemonade and sugar. Refrigerate until ready to serve. Pour over ice and garnish with slice of lemon and sprig of mint!

Note from Melanie: This is the only bagged tea I serve in Miss Melanie's tea room and I use it specifically for our iced tea. Don't have Luzianne at your grocery store? Go to www. Luzianne.com to order yours! I promise I'm not their spokesperson, but you just can't beat this tea.

Green Tea Soaking Salts

He knew we would discuss this another time. A good soak in our antique deep claw foot tub could change any mood. I would just add a couple scoops of our aromatherapy line of green tea soaking salts with chamomile, lavender and peppermint and all my troubles and worries would be forgotten. Light a jasmine white tea candle, grab my favorite book and I would be set for relaxation! It was just what I needed. Amelia Spencer—Chapter Three

1 cups sea salt
2 Tablespoons finely ground Sencha green tea
2 Tablespoons finely ground chamomile
2 Tablespoons finely ground lavender
2 Tablespoons finely ground mint leaves
12 drops lavender essential oil

Place salt in a glass or stainless steel bowl. Grind up spices with a spice or coffee bean grinder dedicated to aromatherapy only as this will interfere with flavors and aroma. Add essential oil and combine with a stainless steel whisk. Place in a glass jar with airtight lid. Store in cool, dry area.

Note from Melanie: To avoid a bit of a mess in your tub, fill cheese cloth, a fabric sachet or t-sac paper filter with tea salts. Drape from faucet and fill your tub with hot water. Now Relax! Tea bath salts can be customized with rose petals, white tea, and any combination of essential oils. Makes wonderful gifts!

Resource Guide

Here is a list of places to visit on the web or when you are visiting Dallas, Texas. I hope you will have fun creating your own "tea adventure" with these wonderful sights!

Smoky Mountain Coffee, Herb & Tea Company
> Official tea company of The Traveling Tea Ladies
> www.SmokyMountainCoffee-Herb-Tea.com
> (423) 926-0123

Southern Methodist University
> Dallas, Texas www.smu.edu

Adolphus Hotel
> 1321 Commerce Street, Dallas, TX 75202
> www.hoteladolphus.com (214)742-8200

The French Room at the Adolphus Hotel
> Afternoon Tea Thurs-Sat 3:00-4:45
> For afternoon tea reservations (214) 742-8200 ext. 3174

Snuffer's
> 3526 Greenville Avenue, Dallas, TX. Best burgers and cheese fries ever!
> www.Snuffers.com (214) 826-6850

Spa Habitat

Voted "Best Spa in Dallas"

3669 McKinney Avenue, Dallas, TX 75204.

www.SpaHabitat.com (214) 522-9989

SMU Marching Jazz Band

"Best Dressed Band in the Land!"

http://people.smu.edu/band/Traditions.htm

Bubba's Chicken

6617 Hillcrest Blvd. Dallas, TX 75205

www.Bubbascatering.org (214) 373-6527

Fans of the Traveling Tea Ladies

Keep up-to-date with book signings, tea tours, recipes and more!

www.TheTravelingTeaLadies.com and

www.Facebook.com//FansOfTheTravelingTeaLadies

La Madeleine's

3072 Mockingbird Lane, Dallas, TX 75205

www.LaMadeleine.com (214) 696-0800

Dakota's Restaurant

600 North Akard Street, Dallas, TX 75201

www.DakotasRestaurant.com (214) 740-4001

The Rosewood Crescent Hotel

400 Crescent Court Dallas, Texas 75201

www.crescentcourt.com (214) 871-3200

About the Author

 Former tea room owner, Melanie O'Hara, is a graduate of Southern Methodist University and East Tennessee State University. Her love of tea was ignited after a semester abroad studying international communications in London, England.

She shares her passion with people inspired to follow their tea dreams through her Tea Academy classes and tea tours.

Melanie, her husband Keith and their brood of children make their home in East Tennessee. When she is not writing, conducting a tea lecture, giving a cooking with tea demonstration or leading a tea tour, you can find her at the helm of her online business, Smoky Mountain Coffee, Herb & Tea Company.

For more information about The Tea Academy, booking your own tea tour, or attending a tea class, e-mail Melanie.

Melanie@TheTravelingTeaLadies.com

And join her tea adventure on Facebook where the tea party never ends!

THE TEA ACADEMY

Consulting & Training for Tea Professionals

www.TheTeaAcademy.com

www.SmokyMountainCoffee-Herb-Tea.com

Official Tea Company of *The Traveling Tea Ladies*

**LYONS
LEGACY
PUBLISHING**™

Traveling Tea Ladies readers, for other Lyons Legacy titles
you may enjoy, or to purchase other books in The Traveling
Tea Ladies Series, signed by the author, visit our website:

www.LyonsLegacyPublishing.com

Love the teas and coffees described in this book? Would you like to purchase more books in the series? Shop with us online!

www.TheTravelingTeaLadies.com

theTraveling
Tea Ladies™

Gourmet Teas, Organic Coffees,
Autographed Books, Gift Baskets
& Apparel

Follow Us On Facebook